The Heritage of Literature Series

ANIMAL FARM

The Heritage of Literature Series

Founder General Editor: E.W. Parker, M.C.

The titles in this series include modern classics, and a wide range of novels, short stories and drama

A selection from the series includes

ANIMAL FARM *George Orwell*
THE WESKER TRILOGY *Arnold Wesker*
THE ROYAL HUNT OF THE SUN *Peter Shaffer*
ROOTS *Arnold Wesker*
SUNSET SONG *Lewis Grassic Gibbon*
THE LONELINESS OF THE LONG-DISTANCE RUNNER *Alan Sillitoe*
  BILLY LIAR *Keith Waterhouse* (in one volume)
THE WORLD OF THE SHORT STORY An anthology chosen by
  A.H.M. Best and M.J. Cohen
FARMER'S BOY *John R. Allan*
MISTER JOHNSON *Joyce Cary*
BRAVE NEW WORLD *Aldous Huxley*

A complete list of the series is available on request

Animal Farm

A Fairy Story by

GEORGE ORWELL

with Introduction and Notes by
Laurence Brander

LONGMAN

LONGMAN GROUP LIMITED
Longman House
Burnt Mill, Harlow, Essex CM20 2JE, England

Acknowledgement

We are indebted to Penguin Books Ltd for permission
to quote lines from Nevill Coghill's translation of
The Canterbury Tales

Eighteenth impression 1981

ISBN O 582 34845 5

First published in the Heritage of Literature Series 1960 by
permission of Messrs Secker and Warburg

Printed in Singapore by
Huntsmen Offset Printing Pte Ltd

CONTENTS

CHAPTER 1

MR. JONES, of the Manor Farm, had locked the hen-houses for the night, but was too drunk to remember to shut the pop-holes. With the ring of light from his lantern dancing from side to side, he lurched across the yard, kicking off his boots at the back door, drew himself a last glass of beer from the barrel in the scullery, and made his way up to bed, where Mrs. Jones was already snoring.

As soon as the light in the bedroom went out there was a stirring and a fluttering all through the farm buildings. Word had gone round during the day that old Major, the prize Middle White boar, had had a strange dream on the previous night and wished to communicate it to the other animals. It had been agreed that they should all meet in the big barn as soon as Mr. Jones was safely out of the way. Old Major (so he was always called, though the name under which he had been exhibited was Willingdon Beauty) was so highly regarded on the farm that everyone was quite ready to lose an hour's sleep in order to hear what he had to say.

At one end of the big barn, on a sort of raised platform, Major was already ensconced on his bed of straw, under a lantern which hung from a beam. He was twelve years old and had lately grown rather stout, but he was still a majestic looking pig, with a wise and benevolent appearance in spite of the fact that his tushes had never been cut. Before long the other animals began to arrive and make themselves comfortable after their different fashions. First came the three dogs, Bluebell, Jessie, and Pitcher, and then the pigs who settled down in the straw immediately in front of the platform. The hens perched themselves on the window-sills, the pigeons fluttered up to the rafters, the sheep and cows lay down behind the pigs and began to chew the cud. The two cart-horses, Boxer and Clover, came in together, walking very slowly and setting down their vast hairy hoofs with great care lest there should be some small animal concealed in the straw. Clover was a stout motherly mare approaching middle life, who had never quite got her figure back after her fourth foal. Boxer was an enormous beast, nearly eighteen hands high, and as strong as any two ordinary horses put together. A white stripe down his nose gave him a somewhat stupid appearance, and in fact he was not of first-rate intelligence, but he was universally respected for his steadiness of character and tremendous powers of work. After the horses came Muriel, the white goat, and Benjamin, the donkey. Benjamin was the oldest animal on the farm, and the worst tempered. He seldom talked, and when he did it was usually to make some cynical remark—for instance, he would say that God had given him a tail to keep the flies off, but that he would sooner have had no tail and no flies. Alone among the animals on the farm he never laughed. If asked why, he would say that he saw nothing to laugh at. Nevertheless, without openly admitting it, he was devoted to Boxer; the two of them usually spent their Sundays together in the small paddock beyond the orchard, grazing side by side and never speaking.

The two horses had just lain down when a brood of ducklings, which had lost their mother, filed into the barn, cheeping feebly and wandering from side to side to find some place where they would not be trodden on. Clover made a sort of wall round them with her great foreleg, and the ducklings nestled down inside it, and promptly fell asleep. At the last moment Mollie, the foolish, pretty white mare who drew Mr. Jones's trap, came mincing daintily in, chewing at a lump of sugar. She took a place near the front and began flirting her white mane, hoping to draw attention to the red ribbons it was plaited with. Last of all came the cat, who looked round, as usual, for the warmest place, and finally squeezed herself in between Boxer and Clover; there she purred contentedly throughout Major's speech without listening to a word of what he was saying.

All the animals were now present except Moses, the tame raven, who slept on a perch behind the back door. When Major saw that they had all made themselves comfortable and were waiting attentively, he cleared his throat and began:

'Comrades, you have heard already about the strange dream that I had last night. But I will come to the dream later. I have something else to say first. I do not think, comrades, that I shall be with you for many months longer, and before I die I feel it my duty to pass on to you such wisdom as I have acquired. I have had a long life, I have had much time for thought as I lay alone in my stall, and I think I may say that I understand the nature of life on this earth as well as any animal now living. It is about this that I wish to speak to you.

'Now, comrades, what is the nature of this life of ours? Let us face it: our lives are miserable, laborious, and short. We are born, we are given just so much food as will keep the breath in our bodies, and those of us who are capable of it are forced to work to the last atom of our strength; and the very instant that our usefulness has come to an end we are slaughtered with hideous cruelty. No animal in England knows the meaning of happiness or leisure after he is a year old. No animal in England is free. The life of an animal is misery and slavery: that is the plain truth.

'But is this simply part of the order of nature? Is it because this land of ours is so poor that it cannot afford a decent life to those who dwell upon it? No, comrades, a thousand times no! The soil of England is fertile, its climate is good, it is capable of affording food in abundance to an enormously greater number of animals than now inhabit it. This single farm of ours would support a dozen horses, twenty cows, hundreds of sheep—and all of them living in a comfort and a dignity that

3

are now almost beyond our imagining. Why then do we continue in this miserable condition? Because nearly the whole of the produce of our labour is stolen from us by human beings. There, comrades, is the answer to all our problems. It is summed up in a single word—Man. Man is the only real enemy we have. Remove Man from the scene, and the root cause of hunger and overwork is abolished for ever.

'Man is the only creature that consumes without producing. He does not give milk, he does not lay eggs, he is too weak to pull the plough, he cannot run fast enough to catch rabbits. Yet he is lord of all the animals. He sets them to work, he gives back to them the bare minimum that will prevent them from starving, and the rest he keeps for himself. Our labour tills the soil, our dung fertilizes it, and yet there is not one of us that owns more than his bare skin. You cows that I see before me, how many thousands of gallons of milk have you given during this last year? And what has happened to that milk which should have been breeding up sturdy calves? Every drop of it has gone down the throats of our enemies. And you hens, how many eggs have you laid this year, and how many of those eggs ever hatched into chickens? The rest have all gone to market to bring in money for Jones and his men. And you, Clover, where are those four foals you bore, who should have been the support and pleasure of your old age? Each was sold at a year old—you will never see one of them again. In return for your four confinements and all your labour in the field, what have you ever had except your bare rations and a stall?

'And even the miserable lives we lead are not allowed to reach their natural span. For myself I do not grumble, for I am one of the lucky ones. I am twelve years old and have had over four hundred children. Such is the natural life of a pig. But no animal escapes the cruel knife in the end. You young porkers who are sitting in front of me, every one of you will scream your lives out at the block within a year. To that

horror we all must come—cows, pigs, hens, sheep, everyone.
Even the horses and the dogs have no better fate. You, Boxer,
the very day that those great muscles of yours lose their power,
Jones will sell you to the knacker, who will cut your throat
and boil you down for the fox-hounds. As for the dogs, when
they grow old and toothless, Jones ties a brick round their
necks and drowns them in the nearest pond.

'Is it not crystal clear, then, comrades, that all the evils of
this life of ours spring from the tyranny of human beings?
Only get rid of Man, and the produce of our labour would be
our own. Almost overnight we could become rich and free.
What then must we do? Why, work night and day, body and
soul, for the overthrow of the human race! That is my message
to you, comrades: Rebellion! I do not know when that
Rebellion will come, it might be in a week or in a hundred
years, but I know, as surely as I see this straw beneath my
feet, that sooner or later justice will be done. Fix your eyes
on that, comrades, throughout the short remainder of your
lives! And above all, pass on this message of mine to those
who come after you, so that future generations shall carry on
the struggle until it is victorious.

'And remember, comrades, your resolution must never
falter. No argument must lead you astray. Never listen when
they tell you that Man and the animals have a common interest,
that the prosperity of the one is the prosperity of the others. It
is all lies. Man serves the interests of no creature except himself.
And among us animals let there be perfect unity, perfect comradeship in the struggle. All men are enemies. All animals
are comrades.'

At this moment there was a tremendous uproar. While
Major was speaking four large rats had crept out of their
holes and were sitting on their hindquarters listening to him.
The dogs had suddenly caught sight of them, and it was only
by a swift dash for their holes that the rats saved their lives.
Major raised his trotter for silence.

'Comrades,' he said, 'here is a point that must be settled. The wild creatures, such as rats and rabbits—are they our friends or our enemies? Let us put it to the vote. I propose this question to the meeting: Are rats comrades?'

The vote was taken at once, and it was agreed by an overwhelming majority that rats were comrades. There were only four dissentients, the three dogs and the cat, who was afterwards discovered to have voted on both sides. Major continued:

'I have little more to say. I merely repeat, remember always your duty of enmity towards Man and all his ways. Whatever goes upon two legs, is an enemy. Whatever goes upon four legs, or has wings, is a friend. And remember also that in fighting against Man, we must not come to resemble him. Even when you have conquered him, do not adopt his vices. No animal must ever live in a house, or sleep in a bed, or wear clothes, or drink alcohol, or smoke tobacco, or touch money, or engage in trade. All the habits of Man are evil. And, above all, no animal must ever tyrannize over his own kind. Weak or strong, clever or simple, we are all brothers. No animal must ever kill any other animal. All animals are equal.

'And now, comrades, I will tell you about my dream of last night. I cannot describe that dream to you. It was a dream of the earth as it will be when Man has vanished. But it reminded me of something that I had long forgotten. Many years ago, when I was a little pig, my mother and the other sows used to sing an old song of which they knew only the tune and the first three words. I had known that tune in my infancy, but it had long since passed out of my mind. Last night, however, it came back to me in my dream. And what is more, the words of the song also came back—words, I am certain, which were sung by the animals of long ago and have been lost to memory for generations. I will sing you that song now, comrades. I am old and my voice is hoarse, but when I have taught you the tune, you can sing it better for yourselves. It is called "Beasts of England".'

Old Major cleared his throat and began to sing. As he had said, his voice was hoarse, but he sang well enough, and it was a stirring tune, something between 'Clementine' and 'La Cucuracha'. The words ran:

Beasts of England, beasts of Ireland,
Beasts of every land and clime,
Hearken to my joyful tidings
Of the golden future time.

Soon or late the day is coming,
Tyrant Man shall be o'erthrown,
And the fruitful fields of England
Shall be trod by beasts alone.

Rings shall vanish from our noses,
And the harness from our back,
Bit and spur shall rust forever,
Cruel whips no more shall crack.

Riches more than mind can picture,
Wheat and barley, oats and hay,
Clover, beans, and mangel-wurzels
Shall be ours upon that day.

Bright will shine the fields of England,
Purer shall its waters be,
Sweeter yet shall blow its breezes
On the day that sets us free.

For that day we all must labour,
Though we die before it break;
Cows and horses, geese and turkeys,
All must toil for freedom's sake.

7

Beasts of England, beasts of Ireland,
Beasts of every land and clime,
Hearken well and spread my tidings
Of the golden future time.

The singing of this song threw the animals into the wildest excitement. Almost before Major had reached the end, they had begun singing it for themselves. Even the stupidest of them had already picked up the tune and a few of the words, and as for the clever ones, such as the pigs and dogs, they had the entire song by heart within a few minutes. And then, after a few preliminary tries, the whole farm burst out into 'Beasts of England' in tremendous unison. The cows lowed it, the dogs whined it, the sheep bleated it, the horses whinnied it, the ducks quacked it. They were so delighted with the song that they sang it right through five times in succession, and might have continued singing it all night if they had not been interrupted.

Unfortunately, the uproar awoke Mr. Jones, who sprang out of bed, making sure that there was a fox in the yard. He seized the gun which always stood in a corner of his bedroom, and let fly a charge of number 6 shot into the darkness. The pellets buried themselves in the wall of the barn and the meeting broke up hurriedly. Everyone fled to his own sleeping place. The birds jumped on to their perches, the animals settled down in the straw, and the whole farm was asleep in a moment.

CHAPTER 2

THREE nights later old Major died peacefully in his sleep. His body was buried at the foot of the orchard.

This was early in March. During the next three months there was much secret activity. Major's speech had given to the more intelligent animals on the farm a completely new outlook on life. They did not know when the Rebellion predicted by Major would take place, they had no reason for thinking that it would be within their own lifetime, but they saw clearly that it was their duty to prepare for it. The work of teaching and organizing the others fell naturally upon the pigs, who were generally recognized as being the cleverest of the animals. Pre-eminent among the pigs were two young boars named Snowball and Napoleon, whom Mr. Jones was breeding up for sale. Napoleon was a large, rather fierce-looking Berkshire boar, the only Berkshire on the farm, not much of a talker, but with a reputation for getting his own way. Snowball was a more vivacious pig than Napoleon, quicker in speech and more inventive, but was not considered to have the same depth of character. All the other male pigs on the farm were porkers. The best known among them was a small fat pig named Squealer, with very round cheeks, twinkling eyes, nimble movements, and a shrill voice. He was a brilliant talker, and when he was arguing some difficult point he had a way of skipping from side to side and whisking his tail which was somehow very persuasive. The others said of Squealer that he could turn black into white.

These three had elaborated old Major's teachings into a complete system of thought, to which they gave the name of Animalism. Several nights a week, after Mr. Jones was asleep, they held secret meetings in the barn and expounded the principles of Animalism to the others. At the beginning they met with much stupidity and apathy. Some of the animals talked of the duty of loyalty to Mr. Jones, whom they referred to as 'Master', or made elementary remarks such as 'Mr. Jones feeds us. If he were gone, we should starve to death.' Others asked such questions as 'Why should we care what happens after we are dead?' or 'If this rebellion is to happen anyway, what difference does it make whether we work for it or not?', and the pigs had great difficulty in making them see that this was contrary to the spirit of Animalism. The stupidest questions of all were asked by Mollie, the white mare. The very first question she asked Snowball was: 'Will there still be sugar after the Rebellion?'

'No,' said Snowball firmly. 'We have no means of making sugar on this farm. Besides, you do not need sugar. You will have all the oats and hay you want.'

'And shall I still be allowed to wear ribbons in my mane?' asked Mollie.

'Comrade,' said Snowball, 'those ribbons that you are so devoted to are the badge of slavery. Can you not understand that liberty is worth more than ribbons?'

Mollie agreed, but she did not sound very convinced.

The pigs had an even harder struggle to counteract the lies put about by Moses, the tame raven. Moses, who was Mr. Jones's especial pet, was a spy and a tale-bearer, but he was also a clever talker. He claimed to know the existence of a mysterious country called Sugarcandy Mountain, to which all animals went when they died. It was situated somewhere up in the sky, a little distance beyond the clouds, Moses said. In Sugarcandy Mountain it was Sunday seven days a week, clover was in season all the year round, and lump sugar and linseed cake grew on the hedges. The animals hated Moses because he told tales and did not work, but some of them believed in Sugarcandy Mountain, and the pigs had to argue very hard to persuade them that there was no such place.

Their most faithful disciples were the two cart-horses, Boxer and Clover. These two had great difficulty in thinking anything out for themselves, but having once accepted the pigs as their teachers, they absorbed everything that they were told, and passed it on to the other animals by simple arguments. They were unfailing in their attendance at the secret meetings in the barn, and led the singing of 'Beasts of England', with which the meetings always ended.

Now, as it turned out, the Rebellion was achieved much earlier and more easily than anyone had expected. In past years Mr. Jones, although a hard master, had been a capable farmer, but of late he had fallen on evil days. He had become much disheartened after losing money in a lawsuit, and had taken to drinking more than was good for him. For whole days at a time he would lounge in his Windsor chair in the kitchen, reading the newspapers, drinking, and occasionally feeding Moses on crusts of bread soaked in beer. His men were idle and dishonest, the fields were full of weeds, the buildings wanted roofing, the hedges were neglected, and the animals were underfed.

June came and the hay was almost ready for cutting. On Midsummer's Eve, which was a Saturday, Mr. Jones went into Willingdon and got so drunk at the Red Lion that he did not come back till midday on Sunday. The men had milked the cows in the early morning and then had gone out rabbiting, without bothering to feed the animals. When Mr. Jones got back he immediately went to sleep on the drawing-room sofa with the *News of the World* over his face, so that when evening came, the animals were still unfed. At last they could stand it no longer. One of the cows broke in the door of the store-shed with her horns and all the animals began to help themselves from the bins. It was just then that Mr. Jones woke up. The next moment he and his four men were in the store-shed with whips in their hands, lashing out in all directions. This was more than the hungry animals could bear. With one accord, though nothing of the kind had been planned beforehand, they flung themselves upon their tormentors. Jones and his men suddenly found themselves being butted and kicked from all sides. The situation was quite out of their control. They had never seen animals behave like this before, and this sudden uprising of creatures whom they were used to thrashing and maltreating just as they chose, frightened them almost out of their wits. After only a moment or two they gave up trying to defend themselves and took to their heels. A minute later all five of them were in full flight down the cart-track that led to the main road, with the animals pursuing them in triumph.

Mrs. Jones looked out of the bedroom window, saw what was happening, hurriedly flung a few possessions into a carpet bag, and slipped out of the farm by another way. Moses sprang off his perch and flapped after her, croaking loudly. Meanwhile the animals had chased Jones and his men out on to the road and slammed the five-barred gate behind them. And so, almost before they knew what was happening, the Rebellion had been successfully carried through: Jones was expelled, and the Manor Farm was theirs.

For the first few minutes the animals could hardly believe in their good fortune. Their first act was to gallop in a body right round the boundaries of the farm, as though to make quite sure that no human being was hiding anywhere upon it; then they raced back to the farm buildings to wipe out the last traces of Jones's hated reign. The harness-room at the end of the stables was broken open; the bits, the nose-rings, the dog-chains, the cruel knives with which Mr. Jones had been used to castrate the pigs and lambs, were all flung down the well. The reins, the halters, the blinkers, the degrading nosebags, were thrown on to the rubbish fire which was burning in the yard. So were the whips. All the animals capered with joy when they saw the whips going up in flames. Snowball also threw on to the fire the ribbons with which the horses' manes and tails had usually been decorated on market days.

'Ribbons,' he said, 'should be considered as clothes, which are the mark of a human being. All animals should go naked.'

When Boxer heard this he fetched the small straw hat which he wore in summer to keep the flies out of his ears, and flung it on to the fire with the rest.

In a very little while the animals had destroyed everything that reminded them of Mr. Jones. Napoleon then led them back to the store-shed and served out a double ration of corn to everybody, with two biscuits for each dog. Then they sang 'Beasts of England' from end to end seven times running, and after that they settled down for the night and slept as they had never slept before.

But they woke at dawn as usual, and suddenly remembering the glorious thing that had happened, they all raced out into the pasture together. A little way down the pasture there was a knoll that commanded a view of most of the farm. The animals rushed to the top of it and gazed round them in the clear morning light. Yes, it was theirs—everything that they could see was theirs! In the ecstasy of that thought they gambolled round and round, they hurled themselves into the air in great leaps of excitement. They rolled in the dew, they cropped mouthfuls of the sweet summer grass, they kicked up clods of the black earth and snuffed its rich scent. Then they made a tour of inspection of the whole farm and surveyed with speechless admiration the ploughland, the hayfield, the orchard, the pool, the spinney. It was as though they had never seen these things before, and even now they could hardly believe that it was all their own.

Then they filed back to the farm buildings and halted in silence outside the door of the farmhouse. That was theirs too, but they were frightened to go inside. After a moment, however, Snowball and Napoleon butted the door open with their shoulders and the animals entered in single file, walking with the utmost care for fear of disturbing anything. They tiptoed from room to room, afraid to speak above a whisper and gazing with a kind of awe at the unbelievable luxury, at the beds with their feather mattresses, the looking-glasses, the horsehair sofa, the Brussels carpet, the lithograph of Queen Victoria over the drawing-room mantelpiece. They were just coming down the stairs when Mollie was discovered to be missing. Going back, the others found that she had remained behind in the best bedroom. She had taken a piece of blue ribbon from Mrs. Jones's dressing-table, and was holding it against her shoulder and admiring herself in the glass in a very foolish manner. The others reproached her sharply, and they went outside. Some hams hanging in the kitchen were taken out for burial, and the barrel of beer in the scullery was stove in with a kick from Boxer's hoof, otherwise nothing in the house was touched. A unanimous resolution was passed on the spot that the farmhouse should be preserved as a museum. All were agreed that no animal must ever live there.

The animals had their breakfast, and then Snowball and Napoleon called them together again.

'Comrades,' said Snowball, 'it is half past six and we have a long day before us. To-day we begin the hay harvest. But there is another matter that must be attended to first.'

The pigs now revealed that during the past three months they had taught themselves to read and write from an old spelling book which had belonged to Mr. Jones's children and which had been thrown on the rubbish heap. Napoleon sent for pots of black and white paint and led the way down to the five-barred gate that gave on to the main road. Then Snowball (for it was Snowball who was best at writing) took a brush between the two knuckles of his trotter, painted out Manor Farm from the top bar of the gate and in its place painted Animal Farm. This was to be the name of the farm from now onwards. After this they went back to the farm buildings, where Snowball and Napoleon sent for a ladder which they caused to be set against the end wall of the big barn. They explained that by their studies of the past three months the pigs had succeeded in reducing the principles of Animalism to Seven Commandments. These Seven Commandments would now be inscribed on the wall; they would form an unalterable law by which all the animals on Animal Farm must live for ever after. With some difficulty (for it is not easy for a pig to balance himself on a ladder) Snowball climbed up and set to work, with Squealer a few rungs below him holding the paint-pot. The Commandments were written on the tarred wall in great white letters that could be read thirty yards away. They ran thus:

THE SEVEN COMMANDMENTS

1. *Whatever goes upon two legs is an enemy.*
2. *Whatever goes upon four legs, or has wings, is a friend.*
3. *No animal shall wear clothes.*
4. *No animal shall sleep in a bed.*
5. *No animal shall drink alcohol.*
6. *No animal shall kill any other animal.*
7. *All animals are equal.*

It was very neatly written, and except that 'friend' was written 'freind' and one of the 'S's' was the wrong way round, the spelling was correct all the way through. Snowball read it aloud for the benefit of the others. All the animals nodded in complete agreement, and the cleverer ones at once began to learn the Commandments by heart.

'Now, comrades,' said Snowball, throwing down the paint-brush, 'to the hayfield! Let us make it a point of honour to get in the harvest more quickly than Jones and his men could do.'

But at this moment the three cows, who had seemed uneasy for some time past, set up a loud lowing. They had not been milked for twenty-four hours, and their udders were almost bursting. After a little thought, the pigs sent for buckets and milked the cows fairly successfully, their trotters being well adapted to this task. Soon there were five buckets of frothing creamy milk at which many of the animals looked with considerable interest.

'What is going to happen to all that milk?' said someone.

'Jones used sometimes to mix some of it in our mash,' said one of the hens.

'Never mind the milk, comrades,' cried Napoleon, placing himself in front of the buckets. 'That will be attended to. The harvest is more important. Comrade Snowball will lead the way. I shall follow in a few minutes. Forward, comrades! The hay is waiting.'

So the animals trooped down to the hayfield to begin the harvest, and when they came back in the evening it was noticed that the milk had disappeared.

CHAPTER 3

H o w they toiled and sweated to get the hay in! But their efforts were rewarded, for the harvest was an even bigger success than they had hoped.

Sometimes the work was hard; the implements had been designed for human beings and not for animals, and it was a great drawback that no animal was able to use any tool that involved standing on his hind legs. But the pigs were so clever that they could think of a way round every difficulty. As for the horses, they knew every inch of the field, and in fact understood the business of mowing and raking far better than Jones and his men had ever done. The pigs did not actually work, but directed and supervised the others. With their superior knowledge it was natural that they should assume the leadership. Boxer and Clover would harness themselves to the cutter or the horse-rake (no bits or reins were needed in these days, of course) and tramp steadily round and round the field with a pig walking behind and calling out 'Gee up, comrade!' or 'Whoa back, comrade!' as the case might be. And every animal down to the humblest worked at turning the hay and gathering it. Even the ducks and hens toiled to and fro all day in the sun, carrying tiny wisps of hay in their beaks. In the end they finished the harvest in two days' less time than it had usually taken Jones and his men. Moreover, it was the biggest harvest that the farm had ever seen. There was no wastage whatever; the hens and ducks with their sharp eyes had gathered up the very last stalk. And not an animal on the farm had stolen so much as a mouthful.

All through that summer the work of the farm went like clockwork. The animals were happy as they had never conceived it possible to be. Every mouthful of food was an acute positive pleasure, now that it was truly their own food, produced by themselves and for themselves, not doled out to them by a grudging master. With the worthless parasitical human beings gone, there was more for everyone to eat. There was more leisure, too, inexperienced though the animals were. They met with many difficulties—for instance, later in the year, when they harvested the corn, they had to tread it out in the ancient style and blow away the chaff with their breath, since the farm possessed no threshing machine—but the pigs with their cleverness and Boxer with his tremendous muscles always pulled them through. Boxer was the admiration of everybody. He had been a hard worker even in Jones's time, but now he seemed more like three horses than one; there were days when the entire work of the farm seemed to rest upon his mighty shoulders. From morning to night he was pushing and pulling, always at the spot where the work was hardest. He had made an arrangement with one of the cockerels to call him in the mornings half an hour earlier than anyone else, and would put in some volunteer labour at whatever seemed to be most needed, before the regular day's work began. His answer to every problem, every setback, was 'I will work harder!'—which he had adopted as his personal motto.

But everyone worked according to his capacity. The hens and ducks, for instance, saved five bushels of corn at the harvest by gathering up the stray grains. Nobody stole, nobody grumbled over his rations, the quarrelling and biting and jealousy which had been normal features of life in the old days had almost disappeared. Nobody shirked—or almost nobody. Mollie, it was true, was not good at getting up in the morning, and had a way of leaving work early on the ground that there was a stone in her hoof. And the behaviour of the cat was somewhat peculiar. It was soon noticed that when there was work to be done the cat could never be found. She would vanish for hours on end, and then reappear at meal-times, or in the evening after work was over, as though nothing had happened. But she always made such excellent excuses, and purred so affectionately, that it was impossible not to believe in her good intentions. Old Benjamin, the donkey, seemed quite unchanged since the Rebellion. He did his work in the same slow obstinate way as he had done it in Jones's time, never shirking, and never volunteering for extra work either. About the Rebellion and its results he would express no opinion. When asked whether he was not happier now that Jones was gone, he would say only 'Donkeys live a long time. None of you has ever seen a dead donkey,' and the others had to be content with this cryptic answer.

On Sundays there was no work. Breakfast was an hour later than usual, and after breakfast there was a ceremony which was observed every week without fail. First came the hoisting of the flag. Snowball had found in the harness-room an old green tablecloth of Mrs. Jones's, and had painted on it a hoof and a horn in white. This was run up the flagstaff in the farm-house garden every Sunday morning. The flag was green, Snowball explained, to represent the green fields of England, while the hoof and horn signified the future Republic of the

18

Animals which would arise when the human race had been finally overthrown. After the hoisting of the flag all the animals trooped into the big barn for a general assembly which was known as the Meeting. Here the work of the coming week was planned out and resolutions were put forward and debated. It was always the pigs who put forward the resolutions. The other animals understood how to vote, but could never think of any resolutions of their own. Snowball and Napoleon were by far the most active in the debates. But it was noticed that these two were never in agreement: whatever suggestion either of them made, the other could be counted on to oppose it. Even when it was resolved—a thing no one could object to in itself—to set aside a small paddock behind the orchard as a home of rest for animals who were past work, there was a stormy debate over the correct retiring age for each class of animal. The Meeting always ended with the singing of 'Beasts of England', and the afternoon was given up to recreation.

The pigs had set aside the harness-room as a headquarters for themselves. Here, in the evening, they studied blacksmithing, carpentering, and other necessary arts from books which they had brought out of the farmhouse. Snowball also busied himself with organising the other animals into what he called Animal Committees. He was indefatigable at this. He formed the Egg Production Committee for the hens, the Clean Tails League for the cows, the Wild Comrades' Re-education Committee (the object of this was to tame the rats and rabbits), the Whiter Wool Movement for the sheep, and various others, besides instituting classes in reading and writing. On the whole, these projects were a failure. The attempt to tame the wild creatures, for instance, broke down almost immediately. They continued to behave very much as before, and when treated with generosity, simply took advantage of it. The cat joined the Re-education Committee and was very active in it for some days. She was seen one day sitting on a roof and talking to some sparrows who were just out of her reach. She was telling them that all animals were now comrades and that any sparrow who chose could come and perch on her paw; but the sparrows kept their distance. The reading and writing classes, however, were a great success. By the autumn almost every animal on the farm was literate in some degree.

As for the pigs, they could already read and write perfectly. The dogs learned to read fairly well, but were not interested in reading anything except the Seven Commandments. Muriel, the goat, could read somewhat better than the dogs, and sometimes used to read to the others in the evenings from scraps of newspaper which she found on the rubbish heap. Benjamin could read as well as any pig, but never exercised his faculty. So far as he knew, he said, there was nothing worth reading. Clover learnt the whole alphabet, but could not put words together. Boxer could not get beyond the letter D. He would trace out A, B, C, D, in the dust with his great hoof, and then would stand staring at the letters with his ears back, sometimes shaking his forelock, trying with all his might to remember what came next and never succeeding. On several occasions, indeed, he did learn E, F. G, H, but by the time he knew them, it was always discovered that he had forgotten A, B, C, and D. Finally he decided to be content with the first four letters, and used to write them out once or twice every day to refresh his memory. Mollie refused to learn any but the six letters which spelt her own name. She would form these very neatly out of pieces of twig, and would then decorate them with a flower or two and walk round them admiring them.

None of the other animals on the farm could get further than the letter A. It was also found that the stupider animals, such as the sheep, hens, and ducks, were unable to learn the Seven Commandments by heart. After much thought Snowball declared that the Seven Commandments could in effect be reduced to a single maxim, namely: 'Four legs good, two legs bad.' This, he said, contained the essential principle of

Animalism. Whoever had thoroughly grasped it would be safe from human influences. The birds at first objected, since it seemed to them that they also had two legs, but Snowball proved to them that this was not so.

'A bird's wing, comrades,' he said, 'is an organ of propulsion and not of manipulation. It should therefore be regarded as a leg. The distinguishing mark of Man is the *hand*, the instrument with which he does all his mischief.'

The birds did not understand Snowball's long words, but they accepted his explanation, and all the humbler animals set to work to learn the new maxim by heart. FOUR LEGS GOOD, TWO LEGS BAD, was inscribed on the end wall of the barn, above the Seven Commandments and in bigger letters. When they had once got it by heart, the sheep developed a great liking for this maxim, and often as they lay in the field they would all start bleating 'Four legs good, two legs bad! Four legs good, two legs bad!' and kept it up for hours on end, never growing tired of it.

Napoleon took no interest in Snowball's committees. He said that the education of the young was more important than anything that could be done for those who were already grown up. It happened that Jessie and Bluebell had both whelped soon after the hay harvest, giving birth between them to nine sturdy puppies. As soon as they were weaned, Napoleon took them away from their mothers, saying that he would make himself responsible for their education. He took them up into a loft which could only be reached by a ladder from the harness-room, and there kept them in such seclusion that the rest of the farm soon forgot their existence.

The mystery of where the milk went to was soon cleared up. It was mixed every day into the pigs' mash. The early apples were now ripening, and the grass of the orchard was littered with windfalls. The animals had assumed as a matter of course that these would be shared out equally; one day, however, the order went forth that all the windfalls were to be collected and brought to the harness-room for the use of the pigs. At this some of the other animals murmured, but it was no use. All the pigs were in full agreement on this point, even Snowball and Napoleon. Squealer was sent to make the necessary explanation to the others.

'Comrades!' he cried. 'You do not imagine, I hope, that we pigs are doing this in a spirit of selfishness and privilege? Many of us actually dislike milk and apples. I dislike them myself. Our sole object in taking these things is to preserve our health. Milk and apples (this has been proved by Science, comrades) contain substances absolutely necessary to the well-being of a pig. We pigs are brain-workers. The whole management and organization of this farm depend on us. Day and night we are watching over your welfare. It is for *your* sake that we drink that milk and eat those apples. Do you know what would happen if we pigs failed in our duty? Jones would come back! Yes, Jones would come back! Surely, comrades,' cried Squealer almost pleadingly, skipping from side to side and whisking his tail, 'surely there is no one among you who wants to see Jones come back?'

Now if there was one thing that the animals were completely certain of, it was that they did not want Jones back. When it was put to them in this light, they had no more to say. The importance of keeping the pigs in good health was all too obvious. So it was agreed without further argument that the milk and the windfall apples (and also the main crop of apples when they ripened) should be reserved for the pigs alone.

CHAPTER 4

By the late summer the news of what had happened on Animal Farm had spread across half the country. Every day Snowball and Napoleon sent out flights of pigeons whose instructions were to mingle with the animals on neighbouring farms, tell them the story of the Rebellion, and teach them the tune of 'Beasts of England'.

Most of this time Mr. Jones had spent sitting in the tap-room of the Red Lion at Willingdon, complaining to anyone who would listen of the monstrous injustice he had suffered in being turned out of his property by a pack of good-for-nothing animals. The other farmers sympathized in principle, but they did not at first give him much help. At heart, each of them was secretly wondering whether he could not somehow turn Jones's misfortune to his own advantage. It was lucky that the owners of the two farms which adjoined Animal Farm were on permanently bad terms. One of them, which was named Foxwood, was a large, neglected, old-fashioned farm, much overgrown by woodland, with all its pastures worn out and its hedges in a disgraceful condition. Its owner, Mr. Pilkington, was an easy-going gentleman farmer who spent most of his time in fishing or hunting according to the season. The other farm, which was called Pinchfield, was smaller and better kept. Its owner was a Mr. Frederick, a tough, shrewd man, perpetually involved in lawsuits and with a name for driving hard bargains. These two disliked each other so much that it was difficult for them to come to any agreement, even in defence of their own interests.

Nevertheless, they were both thoroughly frightened by the rebellion on Animal Farm, and very anxious to prevent their own animals from learning too much about it. At first they pretended to laugh to scorn the idea of animals managing a

23

farm for themselves. The whole thing would be over in a fortnight, they said. They put it about that the animals on the Manor Farm (they insisted on calling it the Manor Farm; they would not tolerate the name 'Animal Farm') were perpetually fighting among themselves and were also rapidly starving to death. When time passed and the animals had evidently not starved to death, Frederick and Pilkington changed their tune and began to talk of the terrible wickedness that now flourished on Animal Farm. It was given out that the animals there practised cannibalism, tortured one another with red-hot horseshoes, and had their females in common. This was what came of rebelling against the laws of Nature, Frederick and Pilkington said.

However, these, stories were never fully believed. Rumours of a wonderful farm, where the human beings had been turned out and the animals managed their own affairs, continued to circulate in vague and distorted forms, and throughout that year a wave of rebelliousness ran through the countryside. Bulls which had always been tractable suddenly turned savage, sheep broke down hedges and devoured the clover, cows kicked the pail over, hunters refused their fences and shot their riders on to the other side. Above all, the tune and even the words of 'Beasts of England' were known everywhere. It had spread with astonishing speed. The human beings could not contain their rage when they heard this song, though they pretended to think it merely ridiculous. They could not understand, they said, how even animals could bring themselves to sing such contemptible rubbish. Any animal caught singing it was given a flogging on the spot. And yet the song was irrepressible. The blackbirds whistled it in the hedges, the pigeons cooed it in the elms, it got into the din of the smithies and the tune of the church bells. And when the human beings listened to it, they secretly trembled, hearing in it a prophecy of their future doom.

Early in October, when the corn was cut and stacked and

some of it was already threshed, a flight of pigeons came whirling through the air and alighted in the yard of Animal Farm in the wildest excitement. Jones and all his men, with half a dozen others from Foxwood and Pinchfield, had entered the five-barred gate and were coming up the cart-track that led to the farm. They were all carrying sticks, except Jones, who was marching ahead with a gun in his hands. Obviously they were going to attempt the recapture of the farm.

This had long been expected, and all preparations had been made. Snowball, who had studied an old book of Julius Caesar's campaigns which he had found in the farmhouse, was in charge of the defensive operations. He gave his orders quickly, and in a couple of minutes every animal was at his post.

As the human beings approached the farm buildings, Snowball launched his first attack. All the pigeons, to the number of thirty-five, flew to and fro over the men's head and muted upon them from mid-air; and while the men were dealing with this, the geese, who had been hiding behind the hedge, rushed out and pecked viciously at the calves of their legs. However, this was only a light skirmishing manoeuvre, intended to create a little disorder, and the men easily drove the geese off with their sticks. Snowball now launched his second line of attack. Muriel, Benjamin, and all the sheep, with Snowball at the head of them, rushed forward and prodded and butted the men from every side, while Benjamin turned round and lashed at them with his small hoofs. But once again the men, with their sticks and their hobnailed boots, were too strong for them; and suddenly, at a squeal from Snowball, which was the signal for retreat, all the animals turned and fled through the gateway into the yard.

The men gave a shout of triumph. They saw, as they imagined, their enemies in flight, and they rushed after them in disorder. This was just what Snowball had intended. As soon as they were well inside the yard, the three horses, the three cows, and the rest of the pigs, who had been lying in ambush in the cowshed, suddenly emerged in their rear, cutting them off. Snowball now gave the signal for the charge. He himself dashed straight for Jones. Jones saw him coming, raised his gun, and fired. The pellets scored bloody streaks along Snowball's back, and a sheep dropped dead. Without halting for an instant Snowball flung his fifteen stone against Jones's legs. Jones was hurled into a pile of dung and his gun flew out of his hands. But the most terrifying spectacle of all was Boxer, rearing up on his hind legs and striking out with his great iron-shod hoofs like a stallion. His very first blow took a stable-lad from Foxwood on the skull and stretched him lifeless in the mud. At the sight, several men dropped their sticks and tried to run. Panic overtook them, and the next moment all the animals together were chasing them round and round the yard. They were gored, kicked, bitten, trampled on. There was not an animal on the farm that did not take vengeance on them after his own fashion. Even the cat suddenly leapt off a roof on to a cowman's shoulders and sank her claws in his neck, at which he yelled horribly. At a moment when the opening was clear, the men were glad enough to rush out of the yard and make a bolt for the main road. And so within five minutes of their invasion they were in ignominious retreat by the same way as they had come, with a flock of geese hissing after them and pecking at their calves all the way.

All the men were gone except one. Back in the yard Boxer was pawing with his hoof at the stable-lad who lay face down in the mud, trying to turn him over. The boy did not stir.

'He is dead,' said Boxer sorrowfully. 'I had no intention of doing that. I forgot that I was wearing iron shoes. Who will believe that I did not do this on purpose?'

'No sentimentality, comrade!' cried Snowball, from whose

wounds the blood was still dripping. 'War is war. The only good human being is a dead one.'

'I have no wish to take life, not even human life,' repeated Boxer, and his eyes were full of tears.

'Where is Mollie?' exclaimed somebody.

Mollie in fact was missing. For a moment there was great alarm; it was feared that the men might have harmed her in some way, or even carried her off with them. In the end, however, she was found hiding in her stall with her head buried among the hay in the manger. She had taken flight as soon as the gun went off. And when the others came back from looking for her, it was to find that the stable-lad, who in fact was only stunned, had already recovered and made off.

The animals had now reassembled in the wildest excitement, each recounting his own exploits in the battle at the top of his voice. An impromptu celebration of the victory was held immediately. The flag was run up and 'Beasts of England' was sung a number of times, then the sheep who had been killed was given a solemn funeral, a hawthorn bush being planted on her grave. At the graveside Snowball made a little speech, emphasizing the need for all animals to be ready to die for Animal Farm if need be.

The animals decided unanimously to create a military decoration, 'Animal Hero, First Class', which was conferred there and then on Snowball and Boxer. It consisted of a brass medal (they were really some old horse-brasses which had been found in the harness-room), to be worn on Sundays and holidays. There was also 'Animal Hero, Second Class', which was conferred posthumously on the dead sheep.

There was much discussion as to what the battle should be called. In the end, it was named the Battle of the Cowshed, since that was where the ambush had been sprung. Mr. Jones's gun had been found lying in the mud, and it was known that there was a supply of cartridges in the farmhouse. It was decided to set the gun up at the foot of the flagstaff, like a piece of artillery, and to fire it twice a year—once on October the twelfth, the anniversary of the Battle of the Cowshed, and once on Midsummer Day, the anniversary of the Rebellion.

CHAPTER 5

As winter drew on, Mollie became more and more troublesome. She was late for work every morning and excused herself by saying that she had overslept, and she complained of mysterious pains, although her appetite was excellent. On every kind of pretext she would run away from work and go to the drinking pool, where she would stand foolishly gazing at her own reflection in the water. But there were also rumours of something more serious. One day as Mollie strolled blithely into the yard, flirting her long tail and chewing at a stalk of hay, Clover took her aside.

'Mollie,' she said, 'I have something very serious to say to you. This morning I saw you looking over the hedge that divides Animal Farm from Foxwood. One of Mr. Pilkington's men was standing on the other side of the hedge. And—I was a long way away, but I am almost certain I saw this—he was talking to you and you were allowing him to stroke your nose. What does that mean, Mollie?'

'He didn't! I wasn't! It isn't true!' cried Mollie, beginning to prance about and paw the ground.

'Mollie! Look me in the face. Do you give me your word of honour that the man was not stroking your nose?'

'It isn't true!' repeated Mollie, but she could not look Clover in the face, and the next moment she took to her heels and galloped away into the field.

A thought struck Clover. Without saying anything to the

others, she went to Mollie's stall and turned over the straw with her hoof. Hidden under the straw was a little pile of lump sugar and several bunches of ribbon of different colours.

Three days later Mollie disappeared. For some weeks nothing was known of her whereabouts, then the pigeons reported that they had seen her on the other side of Willingdon. She was between the shafts of a smart dogcart painted red and black, which was standing outside a public-house. A fat red-faced man in check breeches and gaiters, who looked like a publican, was stroking her nose and feeding her with sugar. Her coat was newly clipped and she wore a scarlet ribbon round her forelock. She appeared to be enjoying herself, so the pigeons said. None of the animals ever mentioned Mollie again.

In January there came bitterly hard weather. The earth was like iron, and nothing could be done in the fields. Many meetings were held in the big barn, and the pigs occupied themselves in planning out the work of the coming season. It had come to be accepted that the pigs, who were manifestly cleverer than the other animals, should decide all questions of farm policy, though their decisions had to be ratified by a majority vote. This arrangement would have worked well enough if it had not been for the disputes between Snowball and Napoleon. These two disagreed at every point where disagreement was possible. If one of them suggested sowing a bigger acreage with barley, the other was certain to demand a bigger acreage of oats, and if one of them said that such and such a field was just right for cabbages, the other would declare that it was useless for anything except roots. Each had his own following, and there were some violent debates. At the Meetings Snowball often won over the majority by his brilliant speeches, but Napoleon was better at canvassing support for himself in between times. He was especially successful with the sheep. Of late the sheep had taken to bleating 'Four legs good, two legs bad' both in and out of season, and they often interrupted the Meeting with this. It was noticed that they were especially liable to break into 'Four legs good, two legs bad' at the crucial moments in Snowball's speeches. Snowball had made a close study of some back numbers of the *Farmer and Stockbreeder* which he had found in the farmhouse, and was full of plans for innovations and improvements. He talked learnedly about field-drains, silage, and basic slag, and had worked out a complicated scheme for all the animals to drop their dung directly in the fields, at a different spot every day, to save the labour of cartage. Napoleon produced no schemes of his own, but said quietly that Snowball's would come to nothing, and seemed to be biding his time. But of all their controversies, none was so bitter as the one that took place over the windmill.

In the long pasture, not far from the farm buildings, there was a small knoll which was the highest point on the farm. After surveying the ground, Snowball declared that this was just the place for a windmill, which could be made to operate a dynamo and supply the farm with electrical power. This would light the stalls and warm them in winter, and would also run a circular saw, a chaff-cutter, a mangel-slicer, and an electric milking machine. The animals had never heard of anything of this kind before (for the farm was an old-fashioned one and had only the most primitive machinery), and they listened in astonishment while Snowball conjured up pictures of fantastic machines which would do their work for them while they grazed at their ease in the fields or improved their minds with reading and conversation.

Within a few weeks Snowball's plan for the windmill were fully worked out. The mechanical details came mostly from three books which had belonged to Mr. Jones—*One Thousand Useful Things to Do About the House, Every Man His Own Bricklayer,* and *Electricity for Beginners*. Snowball used as his study a shed which had once been used for incubators and had a smooth wooden floor, suitable for drawing on. He was closeted there for hours at a time. With his books held open by a stone, and with a piece of chalk gripped between the knuckles of his trotter, he would move rapidly to and fro, drawing in line after line and uttering little whimpers of excitement. Gradually the plans grew into a complicated mass of cranks and cog-wheels, covering more than half the floor, which the other animals found completely unintelligible but very impressive. All of them came to look at Snowball's drawings at least once a day. Even the hens and ducks came, and were at pains not to tread on the chalk marks. Only Napoleon held aloof. He had declared himself against the windmill from the start. One day, however, he arrived unexpectedly to examine the plans. He walked heavily round the shed, looked closely at every detail of the plans and snuffed at them once or twice, then stood for a little while contemplating them out of the corner of his eye; then suddenly he lifted his leg, urinated over the plans, and walked out without uttering a word.

The whole farm was deeply divided on the subject of the windmill. Snowball did not deny that to build it would be a difficult business. Stone would have to be quarried and built up into walls, then the sails would have to be made and after that there would be need for dynamos and cables. (How these were to be procured, Snowball did not say.) But he maintained that it could all be done in a year. And thereafter, he declared, so much labour would be saved that the animals would only need to work three days a week. Napoleon, on the other hand, argued that the great need of the moment was to increase food production, and that if they wasted time on the windmill they would all starve to death. The animals formed themselves into two factions under the slogans, 'Vote for Snowball and the three-day week' and 'Vote for Napoleon and the full manger'. Benjamin was the only animal who did not side with either faction. He refused to believe either that food would become more plentiful or that the windmill would save work.

31

Windmill or no windmill, he said, life would go on as it had always gone on—that is, badly.

Apart from the disputes over the windmill, there was the question of the defence of the farm. It was fully realized that though the human beings had been defeated in the Battle of the Cowshed they might make another and more determined attempt to recapture the farm and reinstate Mr. Jones. They had all the more reason for doing so because the news of their defeat had spread across the countryside and made the animals on the neighbouring farms more restive than ever. As usual, Snowball and Napoleon were in disagreement. According to Napoleon, what the animals must do was to procure firearms and train themselves in the use of them. According to Snowball, they must send out more and more pigeons and stir up rebellion among the animals on the other farms. The one argued that if they could not defend themselves they were bound to be conquered, the other argued that if rebellions happened everywhere they would have no need to defend themselves. The animals listened first to Napoleon, then to Snowball, and could not make up their minds which was right; indeed, they always found themselves in agreement with the one who was speaking at the moment.

At last the day came when Snowball's plans were completed. At the Meeting on the following Sunday the question of whether or not to begin work on the windmill was to be put to the vote. When the animals had assembled in the big barn, Snowball stood up and, though occasionally interrupted by bleating from the sheep, set forth his reasons for advocating the building of the windmill. Then Napoleon stood up to reply. He said very quietly that the windmill was nonsense and that he advised nobody to vote for it, and promptly sat down again; he had spoken for barely thirty seconds, and seemed almost indifferent as to the effect he produced. At this Snowball sprang to his feet, and shouting down the sheep, who had begun bleating again, broke into a passionate appeal in favour of the windmill. Until now the animals had been about equally divided in their sympathies, but in a moment Snowball's eloquence had carried them away. In glowing sentences he painted a picture of Animal Farm as it might be when sordid labour was lifted from the animals' backs. His imagination had now run far beyond chaff-cutters and turnip-slicers. Electricity, he said, could operate threshing machines, ploughs, harrows, rollers and reapers and binders, besides supplying every stall with its own electric light, hot and cold water, and an electric heater. By the time he had finished speaking, there was no doubt as to which way the vote would go. But just at this moment Napoleon stood up and, casting a peculiar side-long look at Snowball, uttered a high-pitched whimper of a kind no one had ever heard him utter before.

At this there was a terrible baying sound outside, and nine enormous dogs wearing brass-studded collars came bounding into the barn. They dashed straight for Snowball, who only sprang from his place just in time to escape their snapping jaws. In a moment he was out of the door and they were after him. Too amazed and frightened to speak, all the animals crowded through the door to watch the chase. Snowball was racing across the long pasture that led to the road. He was running as only a pig can run, but the dogs were close on his heels. Suddenly he slipped and it seemed certain that they had him. Then he was up again, running faster than ever, then the dogs were gaining on him again. One of them all but closed his jaws on Snowball's tail, but Snowball whisked it free just in time. Then he put on an extra spurt and, with a few inches to spare, slipped through a hole in the hedge and was seen no more.

Silent and terrified, the animals crept back into the barn. In a moment the dogs came bounding back. At first no one had been able to imagine where these creatures came from, but the problem was soon solved: they were the puppies whom Napoleon had taken away from their mothers and reared privately. Though not yet full-grown, they were huge dogs, and as fierce-looking as wolves. They kept close to Napoleon. It was noticed that they wagged their tails to him in the same way as the other dogs had been used to do to Mr. Jones.

Napoleon, with the dogs following him, now mounted on to the raised portion of the floor where Major had previously stood to deliver his speech. He announced that from now on the Sunday morning Meetings would come to an end. They were unnecessary, he said, and wasted time. In future all questions relating to the working of the farm would be settled by a special committee of pigs, presided over by himself. These would meet in private and afterwards communicate their decisions to the others. The animals would still assemble on Sunday mornings to salute the flag, sing 'Beasts of England', and receive their orders for the week; but there would be no more debates.

In spite of the shock that Snowball's expulsion had given them, the animals were dismayed by this announcement. Several of them would have protested if they could have found the right arguments. Even Boxer was vaguely troubled. He set his ears back, shook his forelock several times and tried hard to marshal his thoughts; but in the end he could not think of anything to say. Some of the pigs themselves, however, were more articulate. Four young porkers in the front row uttered shrill squeals of disapproval, and all four of them sprang to their feet and began speaking at once. But suddenly the dogs sitting round Napoleon let out deep, menacing growls, and the pigs fell silent and sat down again. Then the sheep broke out into a tremendous bleating of 'Four legs good, two legs bad!' which went on for nearly a quarter of an hour and put an end to any chance of discussion.

Afterwards Squealer was sent round the farm to explain the new arrangement to the others.

'Comrades,' he said, 'I trust that every animal here appreciates the sacrifice that Comrade Napoleon has made in taking this extra labour upon himself. Do not imagine, comrade, that leadership is a pleasure! On the contrary, it is a deep and heavy responsibility. No one believes more firmly than Comrade Napoleon that all animals are equal. He would be only too happy to let you make your decisions for yourselves. But sometimes you might make the wrong decisions, comrades, and then where should we be? Suppose you had decided to follow Snowball, with his moonshine of windmills—Snowball, who, as we now know, was no better than a criminal?'

'He fought bravely at the Battle of the Cowshed,' said somebody.

'Bravery is not enough,' said Squealer. 'Loyalty and obedience are more important. And as to the Battle of the Cowshed, I believe the time will come when we shall find that Snowball's part in it was much exaggerated. Discipline, comrades, iron discipline! That is the watchword for today. One false step, and our enemies would be upon us. Surely, comrades, you do not want Jones back?'

Once again this argument was unanswerable. Certainly the animals did not want Jones back; if the holding of debates on Sunday mornings was liable to bring him back, then the debates must stop. Boxer, who had now had time to think things over, voiced the general feeling by saying: 'If Comrade Napoleon says it, it must be right'. And from then on he adopted the maxim, 'Napoleon is always right,' in addition to his private motto of 'I will work harder.'

By this time the weather had broken and the spring ploughing had begun. The shed where Snowball had drawn his plans of the windmill had been shut up and it was assumed that the plans had been rubbed off the floor. Every Sunday morning at ten o'clock the animals assembled in the big barn to receive their orders for the week. The skull of old Major, now clean of flesh, had been disinterred from the orchard and set up on a stump at the foot of the flagstaff, beside the gun.

After the hoisting of the flag, the animals were required to file past the skull in a reverent manner before entering the barn. Nowadays they did not sit all together as they had done in the past. Napoleon, with Squealer and another pig named Minimus, who had a remarkable gift for composing songs and poems, sat on the front of the raised platform, with the nine young dogs forming a semicircle round them, and the other pigs sitting behind. The rest of the animals sat facing them in the main body of the barn. Napoleon read out the orders for the week in a gruff soldierly style, and after a single singing of 'Beasts of England', all the animals dispersed.

On the third Sunday after Snowball's expulsion, the animals were somewhat surprised to hear Napoleon announce that the windmill was to be built after all. He did not give any reasons for having changed his mind, but merely warned the animals that this extra task would mean very hard work; it might even be necessary to reduce their rations. The plans, however, had all been prepared, down to the last detail. A special committee of pigs had been at work upon them for the past three weeks. The building of the windmill, with various other improvements, was expected to take two years.

That evening Squealer explained privately to the other animals that Napoleon had never in reality been opposed to the windmill. On the contrary, it was he who had advocated it in the beginning, and the plan which Snowball had drawn on the floor of the incubator shed had actually been stolen from among Napoleon's papers. The windmill was, in fact, Napoleon's own creation. Why, then, asked somebody, had he spoken so strongly against it? Here Squealer looked very sly. That, he said, was Comrade Napoleon's cunning. He had *seemed* to oppose the windmill, simply as a manoeuvre to get rid of Snowball, who was a dangerous character and a bad influence. Now that Snowball was out of the way, the plan could go forward without his interference. This, said Squealer, was something called tactics. He repeated a number of times, 'Tactics, comrades, tactics!' skipping round and whisking his tail with a merry laugh. The animals were not certain what the word meant, but Squealer spoke so persuasively, and the three dogs who happened to be with him growled so threateningly, that they accepted his explanation without further questions.

CHAPTER 6

ALL that year the animals worked like slaves. But they were happy in their work; they grudged no effort or sacrifice, well aware that everything that they did was for the benefit of themselves and those of their kind who would come after them, and not for a pack of idle, thieving human beings.

Throughout the spring and summer they worked a sixty-hour week, and in August Napoleon announced that there would be work on Sunday afternoons as well. This work was strictly voluntary, but any animal who absented himself from it would have his rations reduced by half. Even so, it was found necessary to leave certain tasks undone. The harvest was a little less successful than in the previous year, and two fields which should have been sown with roots in the early summer were not sown because the ploughing had not been completed early enough. It was possible to foresee that the coming winter would be a hard one.

The windmill presented unexpected difficulties. There was a good quarry of limestone on the farm, and plenty of sand and cement had been found in one of the outhouses, so that all the materials for building were at hand. But the problem the animals could not at first solve was how to break up the stones into pieces of suitable size. There seemed no way of doing this except with picks and crowbars, which no animal could use, because no animal could stand on his hind legs. Only after weeks of vain effort did the right idea occur to somebody—namely, to utilize the force of gravity. Huge boulders, far too big to be used as they were, were lying all over the bed of the quarry. The animals lashed ropes round these, and then all together, cows, horses, sheep, any animal that could lay hold of the rope—even the pigs sometimes joined in at critical moments—they dragged them with desperate slowness up the slope to the top of the quarry, where they were toppled over the edge, to shatter to pieces below. Transporting the stone when it was once broken was comparatively simple. The horses carried it off in cart-loads, the sheep dragged single blocks, even Muriel and Benjamin yoked themselves into an old governess-cart and did their share. By late summer a sufficient store of stone had accumulated, and then the building began, under the superintendence of the pigs.

But it was a slow, laborious process. Frequently it took a whole day of exhausting effort to drag a single boulder to the top of the quarry, and sometimes when it was pushed over the edge it failed to break. Nothing could have been achieved without Boxer, whose strength seemed equal to that of all the rest of the animals put together. When the boulder began to slip and the animals cried out in despair at finding themselves dragged down the hill, it was always Boxer who strained himself against the rope and brought the boulder to a stop. To see him toiling up the slope inch by inch, his breath coming fast, the tips of his hoofs clawing at the ground, and his great sides matted with sweat, filled everyone with admiration. Clover warned him sometimes to be careful not to overstrain himself, but Boxer would never listen to her. His two slogans, 'I will work harder' and 'Napoleon is always right', seemed to him a sufficient answer to all problems. He had made arrangements with the cockerel to call him three-quarters of an hour earlier in the morning instead of half an hour. And in his spare moments, of which there were not many nowadays, he would go alone to the quarry, collect a load of broken stone, and drag it down to the site of the windmill unassisted.

The animals were not badly off throughout that summer, in spite of the hardness of their work. If they had no more food than they had had in Jones's day, at least they did not have less. The advantage of only having to feed themselves, and not having to support five extravagant human beings as well, was so great that it would have taken a lot of failures to outweigh it. And in many ways the animal method of doing things was more efficient and saved labour. Such jobs as weeding, for instance, could be done with a thoroughness impossible to human beings. And again, since no animal now stole, it was unnecessary to fence off pasture from arable land, which saved a lot of labour on the upkeep of hedges and gates. Nevertheless, as the summer wore on, various unforeseen shortages began to make themselves felt. There was need of paraffin oil, nails, string, dog biscuits, and iron for the horses' shoes, none of which could be produced on the farm. Later there would also be need for seeds and artificial manure, besides various tools and, finally, the machinery for the windmill. How these were to be procured, no one was able to imagine.

One Sunday morning, when the animals assembled to receive their orders, Napoleon announced that he had decided upon a new policy. From now onwards Animal Farm would engage in trade with the neighbouring farms: not, of course, for any commercial purpose, but simply in order to obtain certain materials which were urgently necessary. The needs of the windmill must override everything else, he said. He was therefore making arrangements to sell a stack of hay and part of the current year's wheat crop, and later on, if more money were needed, it would have to be made up by the sale of eggs, for which there was always a market in Willingdon. The hens, said Napoleon, should welcome this sacrifice as their own special contribution towards the building of the windmill.

Once again the animals were conscious of a vague uneasiness. Never to have any dealings with human beings, never to engage in trade, never to make use of money—had not these been among the earliest resolutions passed at that first triumphant Meeting after Jones was expelled? All the animals remembered passing such resolutions: or at least they thought that they remembered it. The four young pigs who had protested when Napoleon abolished the Meetings raised their voices timidly, but they were promptly silenced by a tremendous growling from the dogs. Then, as usual, the sheep broke into 'Four legs good, two legs bad!' and the momentary awkwardness was smoothed over. Finally Napoleon raised his trotter for silence and announced that he had already made all the arrangements. There would be no need for any of the animals to come in contact with human beings, which would clearly be most undesirable. He intended to take the whole burden upon his own shoulders. A Mr. Whymper, a solicitor living in Willingdon, had agreed to act as intermediary between Animal Farm and the outside world, and would visit the farm every Monday morning to receive his instructions. Napoleon ended his speech with his usual cry of 'Long live Animal Farm!', and after the singing of 'Beasts of England' the animals were dismissed.

Afterwards Squealer made a round of the farm and set the animals' minds at rest. He assured them that the resolution against engaging in trade and using money had never been passed, or even suggested. It was pure imagination, probably traceable in the beginning to lies circulated by Snowball. A few animals still felt faintly doubtful, but Squealer asked them shrewdly, 'Are you certain that this is not something that you have dreamed, comrades? Have you any record of such a resolution? Is it written down anywhere?' And since it was certainly true that nothing of the kind existed in writing, the animals were satisfied that they had been mistaken.

Every Monday Mr. Whymper visited the farm as had been arranged. He was a sly-looking little man with side whiskers, a solicitor in a very small way of business, but sharp enough to have realized earlier than anyone else that Animal Farm would need a broker and that the commissions would be worth having. The animals watched his coming and going with a kind of dread, and avoided him as much as possible. Nevertheless, the sight of Napoleon, on all fours, delivering orders to Whymper, who stood on two legs, roused their pride and partly reconciled them to the new arrangement. Their relations with the human race were now not quite the same as they had been before. The human beings did not hate Animal Farm any less now that it was prospering; indeed, they hated it more than ever. Every human being held it as an article of faith that the farm would go bankrupt sooner or later, and, above all, that the windmill would be a failure. They would meet in the public-houses and prove to one another by means of diagrams that the windmill was bound to fall down, or that if it did stand up, then that it would never work. And yet, against their will, they had developed a certain respect for the efficiency with which the animals were managing their own affairs. One symptom of this was that they had begun to call Animal Farm by its proper name and ceased to pretend that it was called the Manor Farm. They had also dropped their championship of Jones, who had given up hope of getting his farm back and gone to live in another part of the country. Except through Whymper, there was as yet no contact between Animal Farm and the outside world, but there were constant rumours that Napoleon was about to enter into a definite business agreement either with Mr. Pilkington of Foxwood or with Mr. Frederick of Pinchfield—but never, it was noticed, with both simultaneously.

It was about this time that the pigs suddenly moved into the farmhouse and took up their residence there. Again the animals seemed to remember that a resolution against this had been passed in the early days, and again Squealer was able to convince them that this was not the case. It was absolutely necessary, he said, that the pigs, who were the brains of the farm, should have a quiet place to work in. It was also more suited to the dignity of the Leader (for of late he had taken to speaking of Napoleon under the title of 'Leader') to live in a house than in a mere sty. Nevertheless, some of the animals were disturbed when they heard that the pigs not only took their meals in the kitchen and used the drawing-room as a recreation room, but also slept in the beds. Boxer passed it off as usual with 'Napoleon is always right!', but Clover, who thought she remembered a definite ruling against beds, went to the end of the barn and tried to puzzle out the Seven Commandments which were inscribed there. Finding herself unable to read more than individual letters, she fetched Muriel.

'Muriel,' she said, 'read me the Fourth Commandment. Does it not say something about never sleeping in a bed?'

With some difficulty Muriel spelt it out.

'It says, "No animal shall sleep in a bed *with sheets*",' she announced finally.

Curiously enough, Clover had not remembered that the Fourth Commandment mentioned sheets; but as it was there on the wall, it must have done so. And Squealer, who happened to be passing at this moment, attended by two or three dogs, was able to put the whole matter in its proper perspective.

'You have heard then, comrades,' he said, 'that we pigs now sleep in the beds of the farmhouse? And why not? You did not suppose surely, that there was ever a ruling against *beds*? A bed merely means a place to sleep in. A pile of straw in a stall is a bed, properly regarded. The rule was against *sheets*, which are a human invention. We have removed the sheets from the farmhouse beds, and sleep between blankets. And very comfortable beds they are too! But not more comfortable than we need, I can tell you, comrades, with all the brainwork we have to do nowadays. You would not rob us of our repose, would

42

you, comrades? You would not have us too tired to carry out our duties? Surely none of you wishes to see Jones back?'

The animals reassured him on this point immediately, and no more was said about the pigs sleeping in the farmhouse beds. And when, some days afterwards, it was announced that from now on the pigs would get up an hour later in the mornings than the other animals, no complaint was made about that either.

By the autumn the animals were tired but happy. They had had a hard year, and after the sale of part of the hay and corn, the stores of food for the winter were none too plentiful, but the windmill compensated for everything. It was almost half built now. After the harvest there was a stretch of clear dry weather, and the animals toiled harder than ever, thinking it well worth while to plod to and fro all day with blocks of stone if by doing so they could raise the walls another foot. Boxer would even come out at nights and work for an hour or two on his own by the light of the harvest moon. In their spare moments the animals would walk round and round the half-finished mill, admiring the strength and perpendicularity of its walls and marvelling that they should ever have been able to build anything so imposing. Only old Benjamin refused to grow enthusiastic about the windmill, though, as usual, he would utter nothing beyond the cryptic remark that donkeys live a long time.

November came, with raging south-west winds. Building had to stop because it was now too wet to mix the cement. Finally there came a night when the gale was so violent that the farm buildings rocked on their foundations and several tiles were blown off the roof of the barn. The hens woke up squawking with terror because they had all dreamed simultaneously of hearing a gun go off in the distance. In the morning the animals came out of their stalls to find that the flagstaff had blown down and an elm tree at the foot of the orchard had been plucked up like a radish. They had just noticed this when a cry of despair broke from every animal's throat. A terrible sight had met their eyes. The windmill was in ruins.

With one accord they dashed down to the spot. Napoleon, who seldom moved out of a walk, raced ahead of them all. Yes, there it lay, the fruit of all their struggles, levelled to its foundations, the stones they had broken and carried so laboriously scattered all around. Unable at first to speak, they stood gazing mournfully at the litter of fallen stone. Napoleon paced to and fro in silence, occasionally snuffing at the ground. His tail had grown rigid and twitched sharply from side to side, a sign in him of intense mental activity. Suddenly he halted as though his mind were made up.

'Comrades,' he said quietly, 'do you know who is responsible for this? Do you know the enemy who has come in the night and overthrown our windmill? SNOWBALL!' he suddenly roared in a voice of thunder. 'Snowball has done this thing! In sheer malignity, thinking to set back our plans and avenge himself for his ignominious expulsion, this traitor has crept here under cover of night and destroyed our work of nearly a year. Comrades, here and now I pronounce the death sentence upon Snowball. "Animal Hero, Second Class", and half a bushel of apples to any animal who brings him to justice. A full bushel to anyone who captures him alive!'

The animals were shocked beyond measure to learn that even Snowball could be guilty of such an action. There was a cry of indignation, and everyone began thinking out ways of catching Snowball if he should ever come back. Almost immediately the footprints of a pig were discovered in the grass at a little distance from the knoll. They could only be traced for a few yards, but appeared to lead to a hole in the hedge. Napoleon snuffed deeply at them and pronounced them to be Snowball's. He gave it as his opinion that Snowball had probably come from the direction of Foxwood Farm.

'No more delays, comrades!' said Napoleon when the footprints had been examined. 'There is work to be done. This very morning we will begin rebuilding the windmill, and we will build all through the winter, rain or shine. We will teach this miserable traitor that he cannot undo our work so easily. Remember, comrades, there must be no alteration in our plans: they shall be carried out to the day. Forward, comrades! Long live the windmill! Long live Animal Farm!'

CHAPTER 7

It was a bitter winter. The stormy weather was followed by sleet and snow, and then by a hard frost which did not break till well into February. The animals carried on as best they could with the rebuilding of the windmill, well knowing that the outside world was watching them and that the envious human beings would rejoice and triumph if the mill were not finished on time.

Out of spite, the human beings pretended not to believe that it was Snowball who had destroyed the windmill: they said that it had fallen down because the walls were too thin. The animals knew that this was not the case. Still, it had been decided to build the walls three feet thick this time instead of eighteen inches as before, which meant collecting much larger quantities of stone. For a long time the quarry was full of snowdrifts and nothing could be done. Some progress was made in the dry frosty weather that followed, but it was cruel work, and the animals could not feel so hopeful about it as they had felt before. They were always cold, and usually hungry as well. Only Boxer and Clover never lost heart. Squealer made excellent speeches on the joy of service and the dignity of labour, but the other animals found more inspiration in

45

Boxer's strength and his never-failing cry of 'I will work harder!'

In January food fell short. The corn ration was drastically reduced, and it was announced that an extra potato ration would be issued to make up for it. Then it was discovered that the greater part of the potato crop had been frosted in the clamps, which had not been covered thickly enough. The potatoes had become soft and discoloured, and only a few were edible. For days at a time the animals had nothing to eat but chaff and mangels. Starvation seemed to stare them in the face.

It was vitally necessary to conceal this fact from the outside world. Emboldened by the collapse of the windmill, the human beings were inventing fresh lies about Animal Farm. Once again it was being put about that all the animals were dying of famine and disease, and that they were continually fighting among themselves and had resorted to cannibalism and infanticide. Napoleon was well aware of the bad results that might follow if the real facts of the food situation were known, and he decided to make use of Mr. Whymper to spread a contrary impression. Hitherto the animals had had little or no contact with Whymper on his weekly visits: now however, a few selected animals, mostly sheep, were instructed to remark casually in his hearing that rations had been increased. In addition, Napoleon ordered the almost empty bins in the store-shed to be filled nearly to the brim with sand, which was then covered up with what remained of the grain and meal. On some suitable pretext Whymper was led through the store-shed and allowed to catch a glimpse of the bins. He was deceived and continued to report to the outside world that there was no food shortage on Animal Farm.

Nevertheless, towards the end of January it became obvious that it would be necessary to procure some more grain from somewhere. In these days Napoleon rarely appeared in public, but spent all his time in the farmhouse, which was guarded at

46

each door by fierce-looking dogs. When he did emerge, it was in a ceremonial manner, with an escort of six dogs who closely surrounded him and growled if anyone came too near. Frequently he did not even appear on Sunday mornings, but issued his orders through one of the other pigs, usually Squealer.

One Sunday morning Squealer announced that the hens, who had just come in to lay again, must surrender their eggs. Napoleon had accepted, through Whymper, a contract for four hundred eggs a week. The price of these would pay for enough grain and meal to keep the farm going till summer came on and conditions were easier.

When the hens heard this, they raised a terrible outcry. They had been warned earlier that this sacrifice might be necessary, but had not believed that it would really happen. They were just getting their clutches ready for the spring sitting, and they protested that to take the eggs away now was murder. For the first time since the expulsion of Jones there was something resembling a rebellion. Led by three young Black Minorca pullets, the hens made a determined effort to thwart Napoleon's wishes. Their method was to fly up to the rafters and there lay their eggs, which smashed to pieces on the floor. Napoleon acted swiftly and ruthlessly. He ordered the hens' rations to be stopped, and decreed that any animal giving so much as a grain of corn to a hen should be punished by death. The dogs saw to it that these orders were carried out. For five days the hens held out, then they capitulated and went back to their nesting boxes. Nine hens had died in the meantime. Their bodies were buried in the orchard, and it was given out that they had died of coccidiosis. Whymper heard nothing of this affair, and the eggs were duly delivered, a grocer's van driving up to the farm once a week to take them away.

All this while no more had been seen of Snowball. He was rumoured to be hiding on one of the neighbouring farms, either Foxwood or Pinchfield. Napoleon was by this time on slightly better terms with the other farmers than before. It happened that there was in the yard a pile of timber which had been stacked there ten years earlier when a beech spinney was cleared. It was well seasoned, and Whymper had advised Napoleon to sell it; both Mr. Pilkington and Mr. Frederick were anxious to buy it. Napoleon was hesitating between the two, unable to make up his mind. It was noticed that whenever he seemed on the point of coming to an agreement with Frederick, Snowball was declared to be hiding at Foxwood, while, when he inclined towards Pilkington, Snowball was said to be at Pinchfield.

Suddenly, early in the spring, an alarming thing was discovered. Snowball was secretly frequenting the farm by night! The animals were so disturbed that they could hardly sleep in their stalls. Every night, it was said, he came creeping in under cover of darkness and performed all kinds of mischief. He stole the corn, he upset the milk-pails, he broke the eggs, he trampled the seed-beds, he gnawed the bark off the fruit trees. Whenever anything went wrong it became usual to attribute it to Snowball. If a window was broken or a drain blocked up, someone was certain to say that Snowball had come in the night and done it, and when the key of the store-shed was lost, the whole farm was convinced that Snowball had thrown it down the well. Curiously enough, they went on believing this even after the mislaid key was found under a sack of meal. The cows declared unanimously that Snowball crept into their stalls and milked them in their sleep. The rats, which had been troublesome that winter, were also said to be in league with Snowball.

Napoleon decreed that there should be a full investigation into Snowball's activities. With his dogs in attendance he set out and made a careful tour of inspection of the farm buildings, the other animals following at a respectful distance. At every few steps Napoleon stopped and snuffed the ground for traces of Snowball's footsteps, which, he said, he could detect by the smell. He snuffed in every corner, in the barn, in the cowshed, in the hen-houses, in the vegetable garden, and found traces of Snowball almost everywhere. He would put his snout to the ground, give several deep sniffs, and exclaim in a terrible voice, 'Snowball! He has been here! I can smell him distinctly!' and at the word 'Snowball' all the dogs let out blood-curdling growls and showed their side teeth.

The animals were thoroughly frightened. It seemed to them as though Snowball were some kind of invisible influence, pervading the air about them and menacing them with all kinds of dangers. In the evening Squealer called them together, and with an alarmed expression on his face told them that he had some serious news to report.

'Comrades!' cried Squealer, making little nervous skips, 'a most terrible thing has been discovered. Snowball has sold himself to Frederick of Pinchfield Farm, who is even now plotting to attack us and take our farm away from us! Snowball is to act as his guide when the attack begins. But there is worse than that. We had thought that Snowball's rebellion was caused by his vanity and ambition. But we were wrong, comrades. Do you know what the real reason was? Snowball was in league with Jones from the very start! He was Jones's secret agent all the time. It has all been proved by documents which he left behind him and which we have only just discovered. To my mind this explains a great deal, comrades. Did we not see for ourselves how he attempted—fortunately without success—to get us defeated and destroyed at the Battle of the Cowshed?'

The animals were stupefied. This was a wickedness far outdoing Snowball's destruction of the windmill. But it was some minutes before they could fully take it in. They all remembered, or thought they remembered, how they had seen Snowball charging ahead of them at the Battle of the Cowshed, how he had rallied and encouraged them at every turn, and how he had not paused for an instant even when the pellets from Jones's gun had wounded his back. At first it was a little difficult to see how this fitted in with his being on Jones's side. Even Boxer, who seldom asked questions, was puzzled. He lay down, tucked his fore-hoofs beneath him, shut his eyes, and with a hard effort managed to formulate his thoughts.

'I do not believe that,' he said. 'Snowball fought bravely at the Battle of the Cowshed. I saw him myself. Did we not give him "Animal Hero, First Class", immediately afterwards?'

'That was our mistake, comrade. For we know now—it is all written down in the secret documents that we have found— that in reality he was trying to lure us to our doom.'

'But he was wounded,' said Boxer. 'We all saw him running with blood.'

'That was part of the arrangement!' cried Squealer. 'Jones's shot only grazed him. I could show you this in his own writing, if you were able to read it. The plot was for Snowball, at the critical moment, to give the signal for flight and leave the field to the enemy. And he very nearly succeeded—I will even say, comrades, he *would* have succeeded if it had not been for our heroic Leader, Comrade Napoleon. Do you not remember how, just at the moment when Jones and his men had got inside the yard, Snowball suddenly turned and fled, and many animals followed him? And do you not remember, too, that it was just at that moment, when panic was spreading and all seemed lost, that Comrade Napoleon sprang forward with a cry of "Death to Humanity!" and sank his teeth in Jones's leg? Surely you remember *that*, comrades?' exclaimed Squealer frisking from side to side.

Now when Squealer described the scene so graphically, it seemed to the animals that they did remember it. At any rate, they remembered that at the critical moment of the battle Snowball had turned to flee. But Boxer was still a little uneasy.

'I do not believe that Snowball was a traitor at the beginning,' he said finally. 'What he has done since is different. But

I believe that at the Battle of the Cowshed he was a good comrade.'

'Our Leader, Comrade Napoleon,' announced Squealer, speaking very slowly and firmly, 'has stated categorically—categorically, comrade—that Snowball was Jones's agent from the very beginning—yes, and from long before the Rebellion was ever thought of.'

'Ah, that is different!' said Boxer. 'If Comrade Napoleon says it, it must be right.'

'That is the true spirit, comrade!' cried Squealer, but it was noticed he cast a very ugly look at Boxer with his little twinkling eyes. He turned to go, then paused and added impressively: 'I warn every animal on this farm to keep his eyes very wide open. For we have reason to think that some of Snowball's secret agents are lurking among us at this moment!'

Four days later, in the late afternoon, Napoleon ordered all the animals to assemble in the yard. When they were all gathered together, Napoleon emerged from the farmhouse, wearing both his medals (for he had recently awarded himself 'Animal Hero, First Class', and 'Animal Hero, Second Class'), with his nine huge dogs frisking round him and uttering growls that sent shivers down all the animals' spines. They all cowered silently in their places, seeming to know in advance that some terrible thing was about to happen.

Napoleon stood sternly surveying his audience; then he uttered a high-pitched whimper. Immediately the dogs bounded forward, seized four of the pigs by the ear and dragged them, squealing with pain and terror, to Napoleon's feet. The pigs' ears were bleeding, the dogs had tasted blood, and for a few moments they appeared to go quite mad. To the amazement of everybody, three of them flung themselves upon Boxer. Boxer saw them coming and put out his great hoof, caught a dog in mid-air, and pinned him to the ground. The dog shrieked for mercy and the other two fled with their tails between their legs. Boxer looked at Napoleon to know whether

51

he should crush the dog to death or let it go. Napoleon appeared to change countenance, and sharply ordered Boxer to let the dog go, whereat Boxer lifted his hoof, and the dog slunk away, bruised and howling.

Presently the tumult died down. The four pigs waited, trembling, with guilt written on every line of their countenances. Napoleon now called upon them to confess their crimes. They were the same four pigs as had protested when Napoleon abolished the Sunday Meetings. Without any further prompting they confessed that they had been secretly in touch with Snowball ever since his expulsion, that they had collaborated with him in destroying the windmill, and that they had entered into an agreement with him to hand over Animal Farm to Mr. Frederick. They added that Snowball had privately admitted to them that he had been Jones's secret agent for years past. When they had finished their confession, the dogs promptly tore their throats out, and in a terrible voice Napoleon demanded whether any other animal had anything to confess.

The three hens who had been the ringleaders in the attempted rebellion over the eggs now came forward and stated that Snowball had appeared to them in a dream and incited them to disobey Napoleon's orders. They, too, were slaughtered. Then a goose came forward and confessed to having secreted six ears of corn during the last year's harvest and eaten them in the night. Then a sheep confessed to having urinated in the drinking pool—urged to do this, so she said, by Snowball—and two other sheep confessed to having murdered an old ram, an especially devoted follower of Napoleon, by chasing him round and round a bonfire when he was suffering from a cough. They were all slain on the spot. And so the tale of confessions and executions went on, until there was a pile of corpses lying before Napoleon's feet and the air was heavy with the smell of blood, which had been unknown there since the expulsion of Jones.

When it was all over, the remaining animals, except for the pigs and dogs, crept away in a body. They were shaken and miserable. They did not know which was more shocking—the treachery of the animals who had leagued themselves with Snowball, or the cruel retribution they had just witnessed. In the old days there had often been scenes of bloodshed equally terrible, but it seemed to all of them that it was far worse now that it was happening among themselves. Since Jones had left the farm, until today, no animal had killed another animal. Not even a rat had been killed. They had made their way on to the little knoll where the half-finished windmill stood, and with one accord they all lay down as though huddling together for warmth—Clover, Muriel, Benjamin, the cows, the sheep, and a whole flock of geese and hens—everyone, indeed, except the cat, who had suddenly disappeared just before Napoleon ordered the animals to assemble. For some time nobody spoke. Only Boxer remained on his feet. He fidgeted to and fro, swishing his long black tail against his sides, and occassionally uttering a little whinny of surprise. Finally he said:

'I do not understand it. I would not have believed that such things could happen on our farm. It must be due to some fault in ourselves. The solution, as I see it, is to work harder. From now onwards I shall get up a full hour earlier in the mornings.'

And he moved off at his lumbering trot and made for the quarry. Having got there, he collected two successive loads of stone and dragged them down to the windmill before retiring for the night.

The animals huddled about Clover, not speaking. The knoll where they were lying gave them a wide prospect across the countryside. Most of Animal Farm was within their view— the long pasture stretching down to the main road, the hay-field, the spinney, the drinking pool, the ploughed fields where the young wheat was thick and green, and the red roofs of the

53

farm buildings with the smoke curling from the chimneys. It was a clear spring evening. The grass and the burst ing hedges were gilded by the level rays of the sun. Never had the farm—and with a kind of surprise they remembered that it was their own farm, every inch of it their own property—appeared to the animals so desirable a place. As Clover looked down the hillside her eyes filled with tears. If she could have spoken her thoughts, it would have been to say that this was not what they had aimed at when they had set themselves years ago to work for the overthrow of the human race. These scenes of terror and slaughter were not what they had looked forward to on that night when old Major first stirred them to rebellion. If she herself had had any picture of the future, it had been of a society of animals set free from hunger and the whip, all equal, each working according to his capacity, the strong protecting the weak, as she had protected the last brood of ducklings with her foreleg on the night of Major's speech. Instead—she did not know why —they had come to a time when no one dared speak his mind, when fierce, growling dogs roamed everywhere, and when you had to watch your comrades torn to pieces after confessing to shocking crimes. There was no thought of rebellion or disobedience in her mind. She knew that, even as things were, they were far better off than they had been in the days of Jones, and that before all else it was needful to prevent the return of the human beings. Whatever happened she would remain faithful, work hard, carry out the orders that were given to her, and accept the leadership of Napoleon. But still, it was not for this that she and all the other animals had hoped and toiled. It was not for this that they had built the windmill and faced the bullets of Jones's guns. Such were her thoughts, though she lacked the words to express them.

At last, feeling this to be in some way a substitute for the words she was unable to find, she began to sing 'Beasts of England'. The other animals sitting round her took it up, and they sang it three times over—very tunefully, but slowly and mournfully, in a way they had never sung it before.

They had just finished singing it for the third time when Squealer, attended by two dogs, approached them with the air of having something important to say. He announced that, by a special decree of Comrade Napoleon. 'Beasts of England' had been abolished. From now onwards it was forbidden to sing it.

The animals were taken aback.

'Why?' cried Muriel.

'It is no longer needed, comrade,' said Squealer stiffly. ' "Beasts of England" was the song of the Rebellion. But the Rebellion is now completed. The execution of the traitors this afternoon was the final act. The enemy both external and internal has been defeated. In "Beasts of England" we expressed our longing for a better society in days to come. But that society has now been established. Clearly this song has no longer any purpose.'

Frightened though they were, some of the animals might possibly have protested, but at this moment the sheep set up their usual bleating of 'Four legs good, two legs bad', which went on for several minutes and put an end to the discussion.

So 'Beasts of England' was heard no more. In its place Minimus, the poet, had composed another song which began:

Animal Farm, Animal Farm,
 Never through me shalt thou come to harm!

and this was sung every Sunday morning after the hoisting of the flag. But somehow neither the words nor the tune ever seemed to the animals to come up to 'Beasts of England'.

CHAPTER 8

A FEW days later, when the terror caused by the executions had died down, some of the animals remembered—or thought they remembered—that the Sixth Commandment decreed: 'No animal shall kill any other animal.' And though no one cared to mention it in the hearing of the pigs or the dogs, it was felt that the killings which had taken place did not square with this. Clover asked Benjamin to read her the Sixth Commandment, and when Benjamin, as usual, said that he refused to meddle in such matters, she fetched Muriel. Muriel read the Commandment for her. It ran: 'No animal shall kill any other animal *without cause*.' Somehow or other, the last two words had slipped out of the animals' memory. But they saw now that the commandment had not been violated; for clearly there was good reason for killing the traitors who had leagued themselves with Snowball.

Throughout that year the animals worked even harder than they had worked in the previous year. To rebuild the windmill, with walls twice as thick as before, and to finish it by the appointed date, together with the regular work of the farm, was a tremendous labour. There were times when it seemed to the animals that they worked longer hours and fed no better than they had done in Jones's day. On Sunday mornings Squealer, holding down a long strip of paper with his trotter, would read out to them lists of figures proving that the production of every class of foodstuff had increased by 200 per cent, 300 per cent, or 500 per cent, as the case might be. The animals saw no reason to disbelieve him, especially as they could no longer remember very clearly what conditions had been like before the Rebellion. All the same, there were days when they felt that they would sooner have had less figures and more food.

All orders were now issued through Squealer or one of the other pigs. Napoleon himself was not seen in public as often as once a fortnight. When he did appear, he was attended not only by his retinue of dogs but by a black cockerel who marched in front of him and acted as a kind of trumpeter, letting out a loud 'cock-a-doodle-doo' before Napoleon spoke. Even in the farmhouse, it was said, Napoleon inhabited separate apartments from the others. He took his meals alone, with two dogs to wait upon him, and always ate from the Crown Derby dinner service which had been in the glass cupboard in the drawing-room. It was also announced that the gun would be fired every year on Napoleon's birthday, as well as on the other two anniversaries.

Napoleon was now never spoken of simply as 'Napoleon'. He was always referred to in formal style as 'our Leader, Comrade Napoleon', and the pigs liked to invent for him such titles as Father of All Animals, Terror of Mankind, Protector of the Sheep-Fold, Ducklings' Friend, and the like. In his speeches, Squealer would talk with the tears rolling down his cheeks of Napoleon's wisdom, the goodness of his heart, and the deep love he bore to all animals everywhere, even and especially the unhappy animals who still lived in ignorance and slavery on other farms. It had become usual to give Napoleon the credit for every successful achievement and every stroke of good fortune. You would often hear one hen remark to another, 'Under the guidance of our Leader, Comrade Napoleon, I have laid five eggs in six days'; or two cows, enjoying a drink at the pool, would exclaim, 'Thanks to the leadership of Comrade Napoleon, how excellent this water tastes!' The general feeling on the farm was well expressed in a poem entitled 'Comrade Napoleon', which was composed by Minimus and which ran as follows:

> *Friend of the fatherless!*
> *Fountain of happiness!*

57

> *Lord of the swill-bucket! Oh, how my soul is on*
> *Fire when I gaze at thy*
> *Calm and commanding eye,*
> *Like the sun in the sky,*
> *Comrade Napoleon!*
>
> *Thou art the giver of*
> *All that thy creatures love,*
> *Full belly twice a day, clean straw to roll upon;*
> *Every beast great or small*
> *Sleeps at peace in his stall,*
> *Thou watchest over all,*
> *Comrade Napoleon!*
>
> *Had I a sucking-pig,*
> *Ere he had grown as big*
> *Even as a pint bottle or a rolling-pin,*
> *He should have learned to be*
> *Faithful and true to thee,*
> *Yes, his first squeak should be*
> *'Comrade Napoleon!'*

Napoleon approved of this poem and caused it to be inscribed on the wall of the big barn, at the opposite end from the Seven Commandments. It was surmounted by a portrait of Napoleon, in profile, executed by Squealer in white paint.

Meanwhile, through the agency of Whymper, Napoleon was engaged in complicated negotiations with Frederick and Pilkington. The pile of timber was still unsold. Of the two, Frederick was the more anxious to get hold of it, but he would not offer a reasonable price. At the same time there were renewed rumours that Frederick and his men were plotting to attack Animal Farm and to destroy the windmill, the building of which had aroused furious jealousy in him. Snowball was known to be still skulking on Pinchfield Farm. In the middle of the summer the animals were alarmed to hear that three hens had come forward and confessed that, inspired by Snowball, they had entered into a plot to murder Napoleon. They were executed immediately, and fresh precautions for Napoleon's safety were taken. Four dogs guarded his bed at night, one at each corner, and a young pig named Pinkeye was given the task of tasting all his food before he ate it, lest it should be poisoned.

At about the same time it was given out that Napoleon had arranged to sell the pile of timber to Mr. Pilkington; he was also going to enter into a regular agreement for the exchange of certain products between Animal Farm and Foxwood. The relations between Napoleon and Pilkington, though they were only conducted through Whymper, were now almost friendly. The animals distrusted Pilkington, as a human being, but greatly preferred him to Frederick, whom they both feared and hated. As the summer wore on, and the windmill neared completion, the rumours of an impending treacherous attack grew stronger and stronger. Frederick, it was said, intended to bring against them twenty men all armed with guns, and he had already bribed the magistrates and police, so that if he could once get hold of the title deeds of Animal Farm they would ask no questions. Moreover, terrible stories were leaking out from Pinchfield about the cruelties that Frederick practised upon his animals. He had flogged an old horse to death, he starved his cows, he had killed a dog by throwing it into a furnace, he amused himself in the evenings by making cocks fight with splinters of razor-blade tied to their spurs. The animals' blood boiled with rage when they heard of these things being done to their comrades, and sometimes they clamoured to be allowed to go out in a body and attack Pinchfield Farm, drive out the humans, and set the animals free. But Squealer counselled them to avoid rash actions and trust in Comrade Napoleon's strategy.

Nevertheless, feeling against Frederick continued to run

high. One Sunday morning Napoleon appeared in the barn and explained that he had never at any time contemplated selling the pile of timber to Frederick; he considered it beneath his dignity, he said, to have dealings with scoundrels of that description. The pigeons who were still sent out to spread tidings of the Rebellion were forbidden to set foot anywhere on Foxwood, and were also ordered to drop their former slogan of 'Death to Humanity' in favour of 'Death to Frederick'. In the late summer yet another of Snowball's machinations was laid bare. The wheat crop was full of weeds, and it was discovered that on one of his nocturnal visits Snowball had mixed weed seeds with the seed corn. A gander who had been privy to the plot had confessed his guilt to Squealer and immediately committed suicide by swallowing deadly night-shade berries. The animals now also learned that Snowball had never—as many of them had believed hitherto—received the order of 'Animal Hero, First Class'. This was merely a legend which had been spread some time after the Battle of the Cowshed by Snowball himself. So far from being decorated, he had been censured for showing cowardice in the battle. Once again some of the animals heard this with a certain bewilderment, but Squealer was soon able to convince them that their memories had been at fault.

In the autumn, by a tremendous, exhausting effort—for the harvest had to be gathered at almost the same time—the windmill was finished. The machinery had still to be installed, and Whymper was negotiating the purchase of it, but the structure was completed. In the teeth of every difficulty, in spite of inexperience, of primitive implements, of bad luck, and of Snowball's treachery, the work had been finished punctually to the very day! Tired out but proud, the animals walked round and round their masterpiece, which appeared even more beautiful in their eyes than when it had been built the first time. Moreover, the walls were twice as thick as before. Nothing short of explosives would lay them low this time! And when they thought of how they had laboured, what discouragements they had overcome, and the enormous difference that would be made in their lives when the sails were turning and the dynamos running—when they thought of all this, their tiredness forsook them and they gambolled round and round the windmill, uttering cries of triumph. Napoleon himself, attended by his dogs and his cockerel, came down to inspect the completed work; he personally congratulated the animals on their achievement, and announced that the mill would be named Napoleon Mill.

Two days later the animals were called together for a special meeting in the barn. They were struck dumb with surprise when Napoleon announced that he had sold the pile of timber to Frederick. Tomorrow Frederick's wagons would arrive and begin carting it away. Throughout the whole period of his seeming friendship with Pilkington, Napoleon had really been in secret agreement with Frederick.

All relations with Foxwood had been broken off; insulting messages had been sent to Pilkington. The pigeons had been told to avoid Pinchfield Farm and to alter their slogan from 'Death to Frederick' to 'Death to Pilkington'. At the same time Napoleon assured the animals that the stories of an impending attack on Animal Farm were completely untrue, and that the tales about Frederick's cruelty to his animals had been greatly exaggerated. All these rumours had probably originated with Snowball and his agents. It now appeared that Snowball was not, after all, hiding on Pinchfield Farm, and in fact had never been there in his life: he was living—in considerable luxury, so it was said—at Foxwood, and had in reality been a pensioner of Pilkington for years past.

The pigs were in ecstasies over Napoleon's cunning. By seeming to be friendly with Pilkington he had forced Frederick to raise his price by twelve pounds. But the superior quality of Napoleon's mind, said Squealer, was shown in the fact that he trusted nobody, not even Frederick. Frederick had wanted to pay for the timber with something called a cheque, which, it seemed, was a piece of paper with a promise to pay written upon it. But Napoleon was too clever for him. He had demanded payment in real five-pound notes, which were to be handed over before the timber was removed. Already Frederick had paid up; and the sum he had paid was just enough to buy the machinery for the windmill.

Meanwhile the timber was being carted away at high speed. When it was all gone, another special meeting was held in the barn for the animals to inspect Frederick's banknotes. Smiling beatifically, and wearing both his decorations, Napoleon reposed on a bed of straw on the platform, with the money at his side, neatly piled on a china dish from the farmhouse kitchen. The animals filed slowly past, and each gazed his fill. And Boxer put out his nose to sniff at the bank-notes, and the flimsy white things stirred and rustled in his breath.

Three days later there was a terrible hullabaloo. Whymper, his face deadly pale, came racing up the path on his bicycle, flung it down in the yard, and rushed straight into the farm-house. The next moment a choking roar of rage sounded from Napoleon's apartments. The news of what had happened sped round the farm like wildfire. The bank-notes were forgeries! Frederick had got the timber for nothing!

Napoleon called the animals together immediately and in a terrible voice pronounced the death sentence upon Frederick. When captured, he said, Frederick should be boiled alive. At the same time he warned them that after this treacherous deed the worst was to be expected. Frederick and his men might make their long-expected attack at any moment. Sentinels were placed at all the approaches to the farm. In addition, four pigeons were sent to Foxwood with a conciliatory message, which it was hoped might re-establish good relations with Pilkington.

The very next morning the attack came. The animals were

at breakfast when the look-outs came racing in with the news that Frederick and his followers had already come through the five-barred gate. Boldly enough the animals sallied forth to meet them, but this time they did not have the easy victory that they had had in the Battle of the Cowshed. There were fifteen men, with half a dozen guns between them, and they opened fire as soon as they got within fifty yards. The animals could not face the terrible explosions and the stinging pellets, and in spite of the efforts of Napoleon and Boxer to rally them, they were soon driven back. A number of them were already wounded. They took refuge in the farm buildings and peeped cautiously out from chinks and knot-holes. The whole of the big pasture, including the windmill, was in the hands of the enemy. For the moment even Napoleon seemed at a loss. He paced up and down without a word, his tail rigid and twitching. Wistful glances were sent in the direction of Foxwood. If Pilkington and his men would help them, the day might yet be won. But at the moment the four pigeons, who had been sent out on the day before, returned, one of them bearing a scrap of paper from Pilkington. On it was pencilled the words: 'Serves you right'.

Meanwhile Frederick and his men had halted about the windmill. The animals watched them, and a murmur of dismay went round. Two of the men had produced a crowbar and a sledge hammer. They were going to knock the windmill down.

'Impossible!' cried Napoleon. 'We have built the walls far too thick for that. They could not knock it down in a week. Courage, comrades!'

But Benjamin was watching the movements of the men intently. The two with the hammer and the crowbar were drilling a hole near the base of the windmill. Slowly, and with an air almost of amusement, Benjamin nodded his long muzzle.

'I thought so,' he said. 'Do you not see what they are doing?

In another moment they are going to pack blasting powder into that hole."

Terrified, the animals waited. It was impossible now to venture out of the shelter of the buildings. After a few minutes the men were seen to be running in all directions. Then there was a deafening roar. The pigeons swirled into the air, and all the animals, except Napoleon, flung themselves flat on their bellies and hid their faces. When they got up again, a huge cloud of black smoke was hanging where the windmill had been. Slowly the breeze drifted it away. The windmill had ceased to exist!

At this sight the animals' courage returned to them. The fear and despair they had felt a moment earlier were drowned in their rage against this vile, contemptible act. A mighty cry for vengeance went up, and without waiting for further orders they charged forth in a body and made straight for the enemy. This time they did not heed the cruel pellets that swept over them like hail. It was a savage, bitter battle. The men fired again and again, and when the animals got to close quarters, lashed out with their sticks and their heavy boots. A cow, three sheep, and two geese were killed, and nearly everyone was wounded. Even Napoleon, who was directing operations from the rear, had the tip of his tail chipped by a pellet. But the men did not go unscathed either. Three of them had their heads broken by blows from Boxer's hoofs; another was gored in the belly by a cow's horn; another had his trousers nearly torn off by Jessie and Bluebell. And when the nine dogs of Napoleon's own bodyguard, whom he had instructed to make a detour under cover of the hedge, suddenly appeared on the men's flank, baying ferociously, panic overtook them. They saw that they were in danger of being surrounded. Frederick shouted to his men to get out while the going was good, and the next moment the cowardly enemy was running for dear life. The animals chased them right down to the bottom of the field, and got in some last kicks at them as they forced their way through the thorn hedge.

They had won, but they were weary and bleeding. Slowly they began to limp back towards the farm. The sight of their dead comrades stretched upon the grass moved some of them to tears. And for a little while they halted in sorrowful silence at the place where the windmill had once stood. Yes, it was gone; almost the last trace of their labour was gone! Even the foundations were partially destroyed. And in rebuilding it they could not this time, as before, make use of the fallen stones. This time the stones had vanished too. The force of the explosion had flung them to distances of hundreds of yards. It was as though the windmill had never been.

As they approached the farm Squealer, who had unaccountably been absent during the fighting, came skipping towards them, whisking his tail and beaming with satisfaction. And the animals heard, from the direction of the farm buildings, the solemn booming of a gun.

'What is that gun firing for?' said Boxer.

'To celebrate our victory!' cried Squealer.

'What victory?' said Boxer. His knees were bleeding, he had lost a shoe and split his hoof, and a dozen pellets had lodged themselves in his hindleg.

'What victory, comrade? Have we not driven the enemy off our soil—the sacred soil of Animal Farm?'

'But they have destroyed the windmill. And we had worked on it for two years!'

'What matter? We will build another windmill. We will build six windmills if we feel like it. You do not appreciate, comrade, the mighty thing that we have done. The enemy was in occupation of this very ground that we stand upon. And now—thanks to the leadership of Comrade Napoleon—we have won every inch of it back again!'

'Then we have won back what we had before,' said Boxer.

'That is our victory,' said Squealer.

They limped into the yard. The pellets under the skin of

Boxer's leg smarted painfully. He saw ahead of him the heavy labour of rebuilding the windmill from the foundations, and already in imagination he braced himself for the task. But for the first time it occurred to him that he was eleven years old and that perhaps his great muscles were not quite what they had once been.

But when the animals saw the green flag flying, and heard the gun firing again—seven times it was fired in all—and heard the speech that Napoleon made, congratulating them on their conduct, it did seem to them after all that they had won a great victory. The animals slain in the battle were given a solemn funeral. Boxer and Clover pulled the wagon which served as a hearse, and Napoleon himself walked at the head of the procession. Two whole days were given over to celebrations. There were songs, speeches, and more firing of the gun, and a special gift of an apple was bestowed on every animal, with two ounces of corn for each bird and three biscuits for each dog. It was announced that the battle would be called the Battle of the Windmill, and that Napoleon had created a new decoration, the Order of the Green Banner, which he had conferred upon himself. In the general rejoicings the unfortunate affair of the bank-notes was forgotten.

It was a few days later than this that the pigs came upon a case of whisky in the cellars of the farmhouse. It had been overlooked at the time when the house was first occupied. That night there came from the farmhouse the sound of loud singing, in which, to everyone's surprise, the strains of 'Beasts of England' were mixed up. At about half past nine Napoleon, wearing an old bowler hat of Mr. Jones's, was distinctly seen to emerge from the back door, gallop rapidly round the yard, and disappear indoors again. But in the morning a deep silence hung over the farmhouse. Not a pig appeared to be stirring. It was nearly nine o'clock when Squealer made his appearance, walking slowly and dejectedly, his eyes dull, his tail hanging limply behind him, and with every appearance of being seriously ill. He called the animals together and told them that he had a terrible piece of news to impart. Comrade Napoleon was dying!

A cry of lamentation went up. Straw was laid down outside the doors of the farmhouse, and the animals walked on tiptoe. With tears in their eyes they asked one another what they should do if their Leader were taken away from them. A rumour went round that Snowball had after all contrived to introduce poison into Napoleon's food. At eleven o'clock Squealer came out to make another announcement. As his last act upon earth, Comrade Napoleon had pronounced a solemn decree: the drinking of alcohol was to be punished by death.

By the evening, however, Napoleon appeared to be some-what better, and the following morning Squealer was able to tell them that he was well on the way to recovery. By the evening of that day Napoleon was back at work, and on the next day it was learned that he had instructed Whymper to purchase in Willingdon some booklets on brewing and dis-tilling. A week later Napoleon gave orders that the small paddock beyond the orchard, which it had previously been intended to set aside as a grazing-ground for animals who were past work, was to be ploughed up. It was given out that the pasture was exhausted and needed re-seeding; but it soon became known that Napoleon intended to sow it with barley.

About this time there occurred a strange incident which hardly anyone was able to understand. One night at about twelve o'clock there was a loud crash in the yard, and the animals rushed out of their stalls. It was a moonlight night. At the foot of the end wall of the big barn, where the Seven Commandments were written, there lay a ladder broken in two pieces. Squealer, temporarily stunned, was sprawling beside it, and near at hand there lay a lantern, a paint-brush, and an overturned pot of white paint. The dogs immediately made a ring round Squealer, and escorted him back to the farmhouse as soon as he was able to walk. None of the animals could form any idea as to what this meant, except old Benjamin, who nodded his muzzle with a knowing air, and seemed to understand, but would say nothing.

But a few days later Muriel, reading over the Seven Commandments to herself, noticed that there was yet another of them which the animals had remembered wrong. They had thought that the Fifth Commandment was 'No animal shall drink alcohol', but there were two words that they had forgotten. Actually the Commandment read: 'No animal shall drink alcohol *to excess.*'

CHAPTER 9

Boxer's split hoof was a long time in healing. They had started the rebuilding of the windmill the day after the victory celebrations were ended. Boxer refused to take even a day off work, and made it a point of honour not to let it be seen that he was in pain. In the evening he would admit privately to Clover that the hoof troubled him a great deal. Clover treated the hoof with poultices of herbs which she prepared by chewing them, and both she and Benjamin urged Boxer to work less hard. 'A horse's lungs do not last for ever,' she said to him. But Boxer would not listen. He had, he said, only one real ambition left—to see the windmill well under way before he reached the age for retirement.

At the beginning, when the laws of Animal Farm were first formulated, the retiring age had been fixed for horses and pigs at twelve, for cows at fourteen, for dogs at nine, for sheep at seven, and for hens and geese at five. Liberal old age pensions had been agreed upon. As yet no animal had actually retired on pension, but of late the subject had been discussed more and more. Now that the small field beyond the orchard had been set aside for barley, it was rumoured that a corner of the large pasture was to be fenced off and turned into a grazing-ground for superannuated animals. For a horse, it was said, the pension would be five pounds of corn a day and, in winter, fifteen pounds of hay, with a carrot or possibly an apple on public holidays. Boxer's twelfth birthday was due in the late summer of the following year.

Meanwhile life was hard. The winter was as cold as the last one had been, and food was even shorter. Once again all rations were reduced, except those of the pigs and dogs. A too rigid equality in rations, Squealer explained, would have been contrary to the principles of Animalism. In any case he had no difficulty in proving to the other animals that they were *not* in reality short of food, whatever the appearances might be. For the time being, certainly, it had been found necessary to make a readjustment of rations (Squealer always spoke of it as a 'readjustment', never as a 'reduction'), but in comparison with the days of Jones, the improvement was enormous. Reading out the figures in a shrill, rapid voice, he proved to them in detail that they had more oats, more hay, more turnips than they had had in Jones's day, that they worked shorter hours, that their drinking water was of better quality, that they lived longer, that a larger proportion of their young ones survived infancy, and that they had more straw in their stalls and suffered less from fleas. The animals believed every word of it. Truth to tell, Jones and all he stood for had almost faded out of their memories. They knew that life nowadays was harsh and bare, that they were often hungry and often cold, and that they were usually working when they were not asleep. But doubtless it had been worse in the old days. They were glad to believe so. Besides, in those days they had been slaves and now they were free, and that made all the difference, as Squealer did not fail to point out.

There were many more mouths to feed now. In the autumn

the four sows had all littered about simultaneously, producing thirty-one young pigs between them. The young pigs were piebald, and as Napoleon was the only boar on the farm, it was possible to guess at their parentage. It was announced that later, when bricks and timber had been purchased, a schoolroom would be built in the farmhouse garden. For the time being, the young pigs were given their instruction by Napoleon himself in the farmhouse kitchen. They took their exercise in the garden, and were discouraged from playing with the other young animals. About this time, too, it was laid down as a rule that when a pig and any other animal met on the path, the other animal must stand aside: and also that all pigs, of whatever degree, were to have the privilege of wearing green ribbons on their tails on Sundays.

The farm had had a fairly successful year, but was still short of money. There were the bricks, sand, and lime for the schoolroom to be purchased, and it would also be necessary to begin saving up again for the machinery for the windmill. Then there were lamp oil and candles for the house, sugar for Napoleon's own table (he forbade this to the other pigs, on the ground that it made them fat), and all the usual replacements such as tools, nails, string, coal, wire, scrap-iron, and dog biscuits. A stump of hay and part of the potato crop were sold off, and the contract for eggs was increased to six hundred a week, so that that year the hens barely hatched enough chicks to keep their numbers at the same level. Rations, reduced in December, were reduced again in February, and lanterns in the stalls were forbidden, to save oil. But the pigs seemed comfortable enough, and in fact were putting on weight if anything. One afternoon in late February, a warm, rich, appetizing scent, such as the animals had never smelt before, wafted itself across the yard from the little brewhouse, which had been disused in Jones's time, and which stood beyond the kitchen. Someone said it was the smell of cooking barley. The animals sniffed the air hungrily and wondered whether a warm mash was being prepared for their supper. But no warm mash appeared, and on the following Sunday it was announced that from now onwards all barley would be reserved for the pigs. The field beyond the orchard had already been sown with barley. And the news soon leaked out that every pig was now receiving a ration of a pint of beer daily, with half a gallon for Napoleon himself, which was always served to him in the Crown Derby soup tureen.

But if there were hardships to be borne, they were partly offset by the fact that life nowadays had a greater dignity than it had had before. There were more songs, more speeches, more processions. Napoleon had commanded that once a week there should be held something called a Spontaneous Demonstration, the object of which was to celebrate the struggles and triumphs of Animal Farm. At the appointed time the animals would leave their work and march round the precincts of the farm in military formation, with the pigs leading, then the horses, then the cows, then the sheep, and then the poultry. The dogs flanked the procession and at the head of all marched Napoleon's black cockerel. Boxer and Clover always carried between them a green banner marked with the hoof and horn and the caption, 'Long live Comrade Napoleon!' Afterwards there were recitations of poems composed in Napoleon's honour, and a speech by Squealer giving particulars of the latest increases in the production of food-stuffs, and on occasion a shot was fired from the gun. The sheep were the greatest devotees of the Spontaneous Demonstration, and if anyone complained (as a few animals sometimes did, when no pigs or dogs were near) that they wasted time and meant a lot of standing about in the cold, the sheep were sure to silence him with a tremendous bleating of 'Four legs good, two legs bad!' But by and large the animals enjoyed these celebrations. They found it comforting to be reminded that, after all, they were truly their own masters and that the work they did was for their own benefit. So that,

71

what with the songs, the processions, Squealer's lists of figures, the thunder of the gun, the crowing of the cockerel, and the fluttering of the flag, they were able to forget that their bellies were empty, at least part of the time.

In April, Animal Farm was proclaimed a Republic, and it became necessary to elect a President. There was only one candidate, Napoleon, who was elected unanimously. On the same day it was given out that fresh documents had been discovered which revealed further details about Snowball's complicity with Jones. It now appeared that Snowball had not, as the animals had previously imagined, merely attempted to lose the Battle of the Cowshed by means of a stratagem, but had been openly fighting on Jones's side. In fact, it was he who had actually been the leader of the human forces, and had charged into battle with the words 'Long live Humanity!' on his lips. The wounds on Snowball's back, which a few of the animals still remembered to have seen, had been inflicted by Napoleon's teeth.

In the middle of the summer Moses the raven suddenly reappeared on the farm, after an absence of several years. He was quite unchanged, still did not work, and talked in the same strain as ever about Sugarcandy Mountain. He would perch on a stump, flap his black wings, and talk by the hour to anyone who would listen. 'Up there, comrades,' he would say solemnly, pointing to the sky with his large beak— 'up there, just on the other side of that dark cloud that you can see—there lies Sugarcandy Mountain, that happy country where we poor animals shall rest for ever from our labours!' He even claimed to have been there on one of his higher flights, and to have seen the everlasting fields of clover and the linseed cake and lump sugar growing on the hedges. Many of the animals believed him. Their lives now, they reasoned, were hungry and laborious; was it not right and just that a better world should exist somewhere else? A thing that was difficult to determine was the attitude of the pigs towards

Moses. They all declared contemptuously that his stories about Sugarcandy Mountain were lies, and yet they allowed him to remain on the farm, not working, with an allowance of a gill of beer a day.

After his hoof had healed up, Boxer worked harder than ever. Indeed, all the animals worked like slaves that year. Apart from the regular work of the farm, and the rebuilding of the windmill, there was the schoolhouse for the young pigs, which was started in March. Sometimes the long hours on insufficient food were hard to bear, but Boxer never faltered. In nothing that he said or did was there any sign that his strength was not what it had been. It was only his appearance that was a little altered; his hide was less shiny than it had used to be, and his great haunches seemed to have shrunken. The others said, 'Boxer will pick up when the spring grass comes on'; but the spring came and Boxer grew no fatter. Sometimes on the slope leading to the top of the quarry, when he braced his muscles against the weight of some vast boulder, it seemed that nothing kept him on his feet except the will to continue. At such times his lips were seen to form the words, 'I will work harder'; he had no voice left. Once again Clover and Benjamin warned him to take care of his health, but Boxer paid no attention. His twelfth birthday was approaching. He did not care what happened so long as a good store of stone was accumulated before he went on pension.

Late one evening in the summer, a sudden rumour ran round the farm that something had happened to Boxer. He had gone out alone to drag a load of stone down to the windmill. And sure enough, the rumour was true A few minutes later two pigeons came racing in with the news: 'Boxer has fallen! He is lying on his side and can't get up!'

About half the animals on the farm rushed out to the knoll where the windmill stood. There lay Boxer, between the shafts of the cart, his neck stretched out, unable even to raise

73

his head. His eyes were glazed, his sides matted with sweat. A thin stream of blood had trickled out of his mouth. Clover dropped to her knees at his side.

'Boxer!' she cried, 'how are you?'

'It is my lung,' said Boxer in a weak voice. 'It does not matter. I think you will be able to finish the windmill without me. There is a pretty good store of stone accumulated. I had only another month to go in any case. To tell you the truth, I had been looking forward to my retirement. And perhaps, as Benjamin is growing old too, they will let him retire at the same time and be a companion to me.'

'We must get help at once,' said Clover. 'Run, somebody, and tell Squealer what has happened.'

All the other animals immediately raced back to the farmhouse to give Squealer the news. Only Clover remained, and Benjamin, who lay down at Boxer's side, and, without speaking, kept the flies off him with his long tail. After about a quarter of an hour Squealer appeared, full of sympathy and concern. He said that Comrade Napoleon had learned with the very deepest distress of this misfortune to one of the most loyal workers on the farm, and was already making arrangements to send Boxer to be treated in the hospital at Willingdon. The animals felt a little uneasy at this. Except for Mollie and Snowball, no other animal had ever left the farm, and they did not like to think of their sick comrade in the hands of human beings. However, Squealer easily convinced them that the veterinary surgeon in Willingdon could treat Boxer's case more satisfactorily than could be done on the farm. And about half an hour later, when Boxer had somewhat recovered, he was with difficulty got on to his feet, and managed to limp back to his stall, where Clover and Benjamin had prepared a good bed of straw for him.

For the next two days Boxer remained in his stall. The pigs had sent out a large bottle of pink medicine which they had found in the medicine chest in the bathroom, and Clover administered it to Boxer twice a day after meals. In the evenings she lay in his stall and talked to him, while Benjamin kept the flies off him. Boxer professed not to be sorry for what had happened. If he made a good recovery, he might expect to live another three years, and he looked forward to the peaceful days that he would spend in the corner of the big pasture. It would be the first time that he had had leisure to study and improve his mind. He intended, he said, to devote the rest of his life to learning the remaining twenty-two letters of the alphabet.

However, Benjamin and Clover could only be with Boxer after working hours, and it was in the middle of the day when the van came to take him away. The animals were all at work weeding turnips under the supervision of a pig, when they were astonished to see Benjamin come galloping from the direction of the farm buildings, braying at the top of his voice. It was the first time that they had ever seen Benjamin excited—indeed, it was the first time that anyone had ever seen him gallop. 'Quick, quick!' he shouted. 'Come at once! They're taking Boxer away!' Without waiting for orders from the pig, the animals broke off work and raced back to the farm buildings. Sure enough, there in the yard was a large closed van, drawn by two horses, with lettering on its side and a sly-looking man in a low-crowned bowler hat sitting on the driver's seat. And Boxer's stall was empty.

The animals crowded round the van. 'Good-bye, Boxer!' they chorused, 'good-bye!'

'Fools! Fools!' shouted Benjamin, prancing round them and stamping the earth with his small hoofs. 'Fools! Do you not see what is written on the side of that van?'

That gave the animals pause, and there was a hush. Muriel began to spell out the words. But Benjamin pushed her aside and in the midst of a deadly silence he read:

'"Alfred Simmonds, Horse Slaughterer and Glue-Boiler, Willingdon. Dealer in Hides and Bone-Meal. Kennels

Supplied." Do you not understand what that means? They are taking Boxer to the knacker's!'

A cry of horror burst from all the animals. At this moment the man on the box whipped up his horses and the van moved out of the yard at a smart trot. All the animals followed, crying out at the tops of their voices. Clover forced her way to the front. The van began to gather speed. Clover tried to stir her stout limbs to a gallop, and achieved a canter. 'Boxer!' she cried. 'Boxer! Boxer! Boxer!' And just at this moment, as though he had heard the uproar outside, Boxer's face, with the white stripe down his nose, appeared at the small window at the back of the van.

'Boxer!' cried Clover in a terrible voice. 'Boxer! Get out! Get out quickly! They are taking you to your death!'

All the animals took up the cry of 'Get out, Boxer, get out!' But the van was already gathering speed and drawing away from them. It was uncertain whether Boxer had understood what Clover had said. But a moment later his face disappeared from the window and there was the sound of a tremendous drumming of hoofs inside the van. He was trying to kick his way out. The time had been when a few kicks from Boxer's hoofs would have smashed the van to matchwood. But alas! his strength had left him; and in a few moments the sound of drumming hoofs grew fainter and died away. In desperation the animals began appealing to the two horses which drew the van to stop. 'Comrades, comrades!' they shouted. 'Don't take your own brother to his death!' But the stupid brutes, too ignorant to realize what was happening, merely set back their ears and quickened their pace. Boxer's face did not reappear at the window. Too late, someone thought of racing ahead and shutting the five-barred gate; but in another moment the van was through it and rapidly disappearing down the road. Boxer was never seen again.

Three days later it was announced that he had died in the hospital at Willingdon, in spite of receiving every attention a horse could have. Squealer came to announce the news to the others. He had, he said, been present during Boxer's last hours.

'It was the most affecting sight I have ever seen!' said Squealer, lifting his trotter and wiping away a tear. 'I was at his bedside at the very last. And at the end, almost too weak to speak, he whispered in my ear that his sole sorrow was to have passed on before the windmill was finished. "Forward, comrades!" he whispered. 'Forward in the name of the Rebellion. Long live Animal Farm! Long live Comrade Napoleon! Napoleon is always right." Those were his very last words, comrades.'

Here Squealer's demeanour suddenly changed. He fell silent for a moment, and his little eyes darted suspicious glances from side to side before he proceeded.

It had come to his knowledge, he said, that a foolish and wicked rumour had been circulated at the time of Boxer's removal. Some of the animals had noticed that the van which took Boxer away was marked 'Horse Slaughterer', and had actually jumped to the conclusion that Boxer was being sent to the knacker's. It was almost unbelievable, said Squealer, that any animal could be so stupid. Surely, he cried indignantly, whisking his tail and skipping from side to side, surely they knew their beloved Leader, Comrade Napoleon, better than that? But the explanation was really very simple. The van had previously been the property of the knacker, and had been bought by the veterinary surgeon, who had not yet painted the old name out. That was how the mistake had arisen.

The animals were enormously relieved to hear this. And when Squealer went on to give further graphic details of Boxer's death bed, the admirable care he had received, and the expensive medicines for which Napoleon had paid without a thought as to the cost, their last doubts disappeared and the sorrow that they felt for their comrade's death was tempered by the thought that at least he had died happy.

Napoleon himself appeared at the meeting on the following

77

Sunday morning and pronounced a short oration in Boxer's honour. It had not been possible, he said, to bring back their lamented comrade's remains for interment on the farm, but he had ordered a large wreath to be made from the laurels in the farmhouse garden and sent down to be placed on Boxer's grave. And in a few days' time the pigs intended to hold a memorial banquet in Boxer's honour. Napoleon ended his speech with a reminder of Boxer's two favourite maxims, 'I will work harder' and 'Comrade Napoleon is always right'— maxims, he said, which every animal would do well to adopt as his own.

On the day appointed for the banquet, a grocer's van drove up from Willingdon and delivered a large wooden crate at the farmhouse. That night there was the sound of uproarious singing, which was followed by what sounded like a violent quarrel and ended at about eleven o'clock with a tremendous crash of glass. No one stirred in the farmhouse before noon on the following day, and the word went round that from somewhere or other the pigs had acquired the money to buy themselves another case of whisky.

CHAPTER 10

YEARS passed. The seasons came and went, the short animal lives fled by. A time came when there was no one who remembered the old days before the Rebellion, except Clover, Benjamin, Moses the raven, and a number of the pigs.

Muriel was dead; Bluebell, Jessie, and Pitcher were dead. Jones too was dead—he had died in an inebriates' home in another part of the country. Snowball was forgotten. Boxer was forgotten, except by the few who had known him. Clover was an old stout mare now, stiff in the joints, and with a tendency to rheumy eyes. She was two years past retiring age, but in fact no animal had ever actually retired. The talk of setting aside a corner of the pasture for superannuated animals had long since been dropped. Napoleon was now a mature boar of twenty-four stone. Squealer was so fat that he could with difficulty see out of his eyes. Only old Benjamin was much the same as ever, except for being a little greyer about the muzzle, and, since Boxer's death, more morose and taciturn than ever.

There were many more creatures on the farm now, though the increase was not so great as had been expected in earlier years. Many animals had been born to whom the Rebellion was only a dim tradition, passed on by word of mouth, and others had been bought who had never heard mention of such a thing before their arrival. The farm possessed three horses now besides Clover. They were fine upstanding beasts, willing workers and good comrades, but very stupid. None of them proved able to learn the alphabet beyond the letter B. They accepted everything that they were told about the Rebellion and the principles of Animalism, especially from Clover, for whom they had an almost filial respect; but it was doubtful whether they understood very much of it.

The farm was more prosperous now, and better organized: it had even been enlarged by two fields which had been bought from Mr. Pilkington. The windmill had been successfully completed at last, and the farm possessed a threshing machine and a hay elevator of its own, and various new buildings had been added to it. Whymper had bought himself a dogcart. The windmill, however, had not after all been used for generating electrical power. It was used for milling corn, and brought in a handsome money profit. The animals were hard at work building yet another windmill; when that one was finished, so it was said, the dynamos would be installed. But the luxuries of which Snowball had once taught the animals to dream, the stalls with electric light and hot and cold water, and the three-day week, were no longer talked about. Napoleon had denounced such ideas as contrary to the spirit of Animalism. The truest happiness, he said, lay in working hard and living frugally.

Somehow it seemed as though the farm had grown richer without making the animals themselves any richer—except, of course, for the pigs and the dogs. Perhaps this was partly because there were so many pigs and so many dogs. It was not that these creatures did not work, after their fashion. There was, as Squealer was never tired of explaining, endless work in the supervision and organization of the farm. Much of this work was of a kind that the other animals were too ignorant to understand. For example, Squealer told them that the pigs had to expend enormous labours every day upon mysterious things called 'files', 'reports', 'minutes', and 'memoranda'. These were large sheets of paper which had to be closely covered with writing, and as soon as they were so covered, they were burnt in the furnace. This was of the highest importance for the welfare of the farm, Squealer said. But still, neither pigs nor dogs produced any food by their own labour; and there were very many of them, and their appetites were always good.

As for the others, their life, so far as they knew, was as it had always been. They were generally hungry, they slept on straw, they drank from the pool, they laboured in the fields; in winter they were troubled by the cold, and in the summer by the flies. Sometimes the older ones among them racked their dim memories and tried to determine whether in the early days of the Rebellion, when Jones's expulsion was still recent, things had been better or worse than now. They could not remember. There was nothing with which they could compare their present lives: they had nothing to go upon except Squealer's lists of figures, which invariably demonstrated that everything was getting better and better. The animals found the problem insoluble; in any case, they had little time for speculating on such things now. Only old Benjamin professed to remember every detail of his long life and to know that things never had been, nor ever could be much better or much worse—hunger, hardship, and disappointment being, so he said, the unalterable law of life.

And yet the animals never gave up hope. More, they never lost, even for an instant, their sense of honour and privilege in being members of Animal Farm. They were still the only farm in the whole country—in all England!—owned and operated by animals. Not one of them, not even the youngest, not even the newcomers who had been brought from farms ten or twenty miles away, ever ceased to marvel at that. And when they heard the gun booming and saw the green flag fluttering at the masthead, their hearts swelled with imperishable pride, and the talk always turned towards the old heroic days, the expulsion of Jones, the writing of the Seven Commandments, the great battles in which the human invaders had been defeated. None of the old dreams had been abandoned. The Republic of the Animals which Major had foretold, when the green fields of England should be untrodden by human feet, was still believed in. Some day it was coming: it might not be soon, it might not be within the lifetime of any animal now living, but still it was coming. Even the tune of 'Beasts of England' was perhaps hummed secretly here and there: at any rate, it was a fact that every animal on the farm knew it, though no one would have dared to sing it aloud. It might be that their lives were hard and that not all of their hopes had been fulfilled; but they were conscious that they were not as other animals. If they were hungry, it was not from feeding tyrannical human beings; if they worked hard, at least they worked for themselves. No creature among them went upon two legs. No creature called any other creature 'Master'. All animals were equal.

One day in early summer Squealer ordered the sheep to follow him, and led them out to a piece of waste ground at

81

the other end of the farm, which had become overgrown with birch saplings. The sheep spent the whole day there browsing at the leaves under Squealer's supervision. In the evening he returned to the farmhouse himself, but, as it was warm weather, told the sheep to stay where they were. It ended by their remaining there for a whole week, during which time the other animals saw nothing of them. Squealer was with them for the greater part of every day. He was, he said, teaching them to sing a new song, for which privacy was needed.

It was just after the sheep had returned, on a pleasant evening when the animals had finished work and were making their way back to the farm buildings, that the terrified neighing of a horse sounded from the yard. Startled, the animals stopped in their tracks. It was Clover's voice. She neighed again, and all the animals broke into a gallop and rushed into the yard. Then they saw what Clover had seen.

It was a pig walking on his hind legs.

Yes, it was Squealer. A little awkwardly, as though not quite used to supporting his considerable bulk in that position, but with perfect balance, he was strolling across the yard. And a moment later, out from the door of the farmhouse came a long file of pigs, all walking on their hind legs. Some did it better than others, one or two were even a trifle unsteady and looked as though they would have liked the support of a stick, but every one of them made his way right round the yard successfully. And finally there was a tremendous baying of dogs and a shrill crowing from the black cockerel, and out came Napoleon himself, majestically upright, casting haughty glances from side to side, and with his dogs gambolling round him.

He carried a whip in his trotter.

There was a deadly silence. Amazed, terrified, huddling together, the animals watched the long line of pigs march slowly round the yard. It was as though the world had turned upside-down. Then there came a moment when the first shock had worn off and when, in spite of everything—in spite of their terror of the dogs, and of the habit, developed through long years, of never complaining, never criticizing, no matter what happened—they might have uttered some word of protest. But just at that moment, as though at a signal, all the sheep burst out into a tremendous bleating of—

'Four legs good, two legs *better*! Four legs good, two legs *better*! Four legs good, two legs *better*!'

It went on for five minutes without stopping. And by the time the sheep had quieted down, the chance to utter any protest had passed, for the pigs had marched back into the farmhouse.

Benjamin felt a nose nuzzling at his shoulder. He looked round. It was Clover. Her old eyes looked dimmer than ever. Without saying anything, she tugged gently at his mane and led him round to the end of the big barn, where the Seven Commandments were written. For a minute or two they stood gazing at the tarred wall with its white lettering.

'My sight is failing,' she said finally. 'Even when I was young I could not have read what was written there. But it appears to me that that wall looks different. Are the Seven Commandments the same as they used to be, Benjamin?'

For once Benjamin consented to break his rule, and he read out to her what was written on the wall. There was nothing there now except a single Commandment. It ran:

ALL ANIMALS ARE EQUAL
BUT SOME ANIMALS ARE MORE
EQUAL THAN OTHERS

After that it did not seem strange when next day the pigs who were supervising the work of the farm all carried whips in their trotters. It did not seem strange to learn that the pigs had bought themselves a wireless set, were arranging to install a telephone, and had taken out subscriptions to *John Bull*, *Tit-*

Bits, and the *Daily Mirror*. It did not seem strange when Napoleon was seen strolling in the farmhouse garden with a pipe in his mouth—no, not even when the pigs took Mr. Jones's clothes out of the wardrobes and put them on, Napoleon himself appearing in a black coat, rat-catcher breeches, and leather leggings, while his favourite sow appeared in the watered silk dress which Mrs. Jones had been used to wear on Sundays.

A week later, in the afternoon, a number of dog-carts drove up to the farm. A deputation of neighbouring farmers, had been invited to make a tour of inspection. They were shown all over the farm, and expressed great admiration for everything they saw, especially the windmill. The animals were weeding the turnip field. They worked diligently, hardly raising their faces from the ground, and not knowing whether to be more frightened of the pigs or of the human visitors.

That evening loud laughter and bursts of singing came from the farmhouse. And suddenly, at the sound of the mingled voices, the animals were stricken with curiosity. What could be happening in there, now that for the first time animals and human beings were meeting on terms of equality? With one accord they began to creep as quietly as possible into the farmhouse garden.

At the gate they passed, half frightened to go on, but Clover led the way in. They tiptoed up to the house, and such animals as were tall enough peered in at the dining-room window. There, round the long table, sat half a dozen farmers and half a dozen of the more eminent pigs, Napoleon himself occupying the seat of honour at the head of the table. The pigs appeared completely at ease in their chairs. The company had been enjoying a game of cards, but had broken off for a moment, evidently in order to drink a toast. A large jug was circulating, and the mugs were being refilled with beer. No one noticed the wondering faces of the animals that gazed in at the window.

Mr. Pilkington of Foxwood, had stood up, his mug in his hand. In a moment, he said, he would ask the present company to drink a toast. But before doing so, there were a few words that he felt it incumbent upon him to say.

It was a source of great satisfaction to him, he said—and, he was sure, to all others present—to feel that a long period of mistrust and misunderstanding had now come to an end. There had been a time—not that he, or any of the present company, had shared such sentiments—but there had been a time when the respected proprietors of Animal Farm had been regarded, he would not say with hostility, but perhaps with a certain measure of misgiving, by their human neighbours. Unfortunate incidents had occurred, mistaken ideas had been current. It had been felt that the existence of a farm owned and operated by pigs was somehow abnormal and was liable to have an unsettling effect in the neighbourhood. Too many farmers had assumed, without due inquiry, that on such a farm a spirit of licence and indiscipline would prevail. They had been nervous about the effects upon their own animals, or even upon their human employees. But all such doubts were now dispelled. Today he and his friends had visited Animal Farm and inspected every inch of it with their own eyes, and what did they find? Not only the most up-to-date methods, but a discipline and an orderliness which should be an example to all farmers everywhere. He believed that he was right in saying that the lower animals on Animal Farm did more work and received less food than any animals in the country. Indeed, he and his fellow-visitors today had observed many features which they intended to introduce on their own farms immediately.

He would end his remarks, he said, by emphasizing once again the friendly feelings that subsisted, and ought to subsist, between Animal Farm and its neighbours. Between pigs and human beings there was not, and there need not be, any clash of interests whatever. Their struggles and their difficulties were one. Was not the labour problem the same everywhere? Here it became apparent that Mr. Pilkington was about to spring some carefully prepared witticism on the company, but for a moment he was too overcome by amusement to be able to utter it. After much choking, during which his various chins turned purple, he managed to get it out: 'If you have your lower animals to contend with,' he said, 'we have our lower classes!' This *bon mot* set the table in a roar; and Mr. Pilkington once again congratulated the pigs on the low rations, the long working hours, and the general absence of pampering which he had observed on Animal Farm.

And now, he said finally, he would ask the company to rise on their feet and make certain that their glasses were full. 'Gentlemen,' concluded Mr. Pilkington, 'gentlemen, I give you a toast: to the prosperity of Animal Farm!'

There was enthusiastic cheering and stamping of feet. Napoleon was so gratified that he left his place and came round the table to clink his mug against Mr. Pilkington's before emptying it. When the cheering had died down, Napoleon, who had remained on his feet, intimated that he too had a few words to say.

Like all Napoleon's speeches, it was short and to the point. He too, he said, was happy that the period of misunderstanding was at an end. For a long time there had been rumours—circulated, he had reason to think, by some malignant enemy—that there was something subversive and even revolutionary in the outlook of himself and his colleagues. They had been credited with attempting to stir up rebellion among the animals on neighbouring farms. Nothing could be further from the truth! Their sole wish, now and in the past, was to live at peace and in normal business relations with their neighbours. This farm which he had the honour to control, he added, was a co-operative enterprise. The title-deeds, which were in his own possession, were owned by the pigs jointly.

He did not believe, he said, that any of the old suspicions still lingered, but certain changes had been made recently in the routine of the farm which should have the effect of promoting confidence still further. Hitherto the animals on the farm had had a rather foolish custom of addressing one another as 'Comrade'. This was to be suppressed. There had also been a very strange custom, whose origin was unknown, of marching every Sunday morning past a boar's skull which was nailed to a post in the garden. This, too, would be suppressed, and the skull had already been buried. His visitors might have observed, too, the green flag which flew from the masthead. If so, they would perhaps have noted that the white hoof and horn with which it had previously been marked had now been removed. It would be a plain green flag from now onwards.

He had only one criticism, he said, to make of Mr. Pilkington's excellent and neighbourly speech. Mr. Pilkington had referred throughout to 'Animal Farm'. He could not of course know—for he, Napoleon, was only now for the first time announcing it—that the name 'Animal Farm' had been abolished. Henceforward the farm was to be known as the 'Manor Farm'—which, he believed, was its correct and original name.

'Gentlemen,' concluded Napoleon, 'I will give you the same toast as before, but in a different form. Fill your glasses to the brim. Gentlemen, here is my toast: To the prosperity of the Manor Farm!'

There was the same hearty cheering as before, and the mugs were emptied to the dregs. But as the animals outside gazed at the scene, it seemed to them that some strange thing was happening. What was it that had altered in the faces of the pigs? Clover's old dim eyes flitted from one face to another. Some of them had five chins, some had four, some had three. But what was it that seemed to be melting and changing? Then, the applause having come to an end, the company took up their cards and continued the game that had been interrupted, and the animals crept silently away.

But they had not gone twenty yards when they stopped short. An uproar of voices was coming from the farmhouse. They rushed back and looked through the window again. Yes, a violent quarrel was in progress. There were shoutings, bangings on the table, sharp suspicious glances, furious denials. The source of the trouble appeared to be that Napoleon and Mr. Pilkington had each played an ace of spades simultaneously.

Twelve voices were shouting in anger, and they were all alike. No question, now, what had happened to the faces of the pigs. The creatures outside looked from pig to man, and from man to pig, and from pig to man again; but already it was impossible to say which was which.

INTRODUCTION

by Laurence Brander

I. GEORGE ORWELL: HIS LIFE AND WRITINGS

GEORGE ORWELL, the author of *Animal Farm*, is one of the great English political satirists. Satire is one of the more intellectual kinds of writing and most modern satirists have lived quiet intellectual lives. Orwell's life was different, as the titles of his books themselves will show: *Burmese Days, Down and Out in Paris and London, The Road to Wigan Pier, Homage to Catalonia.* These titles highlight his adventures. They are all based on description of what he had seen and done. In his last books, in *Animal Farm*, which is his best, and in *1984*, which is his best known, he turned from description and recollection to imaginative creation.

He was born in 1903 in Bengal, where his father was a government official. His name was Eric Blair. George Orwell was a writing name, which he used also in everyday life. Like all English children in India whose parents could afford it, he came home as a small boy to go to his preparatory school. He was accepted with reduced fees as some clever boys were because they would be a good advertisement for the school. This, and his unhappiness at his prep. school, is described in a short autobiography called *Such, Such were the Joys*, which is not yet published in England.

He won scholarships to Eton and Wellington and chose Eton, which in those days indicated that his parents had some money behind them. As a scholar at Eton, it would have been routine to go to Oxford or Cambridge University, especially if he had literary inclinations. Instead, Blair joined the Indian Police and was posted to Burma. The Police Service in India was a fine one, badly paid for difficult and unpleasant work. Orwell served for five years, learning about life at first hand

and a seamy side of it too, while his school friends were reading about it at college.

After five years' service he had earned home leave and, as he tells us, one whiff of English air made up his mind for him that he would never go back to Burma. He had gone as a boy, uncertain how to achieve his ambition in life. He came back a man, quite clear that he was going to be a writer. He must have heard a great deal about India from his family, the kind of talk that makes India the most glamorous country in the world. As it is, but not for a writer. He would never have become a writer as a police official in Burma. Work and climate would have been against him. For a good part of the year it is so hot that serious reading, to say nothing of writing, is impossible.

If young Blair did not become George Orwell the writer in Burma, he did make notes, and these notes were developed eventually into a novel, *Burmese Days*, and two short pieces called *Shooting an Elephant* and *A Hanging*. An artist sees more vividly than other people and young Blair shows this quality in his descriptions of birds and plants and the harsh metallic skies of that hot and sultry land.

That was the first stage of his working life. People who knew him in Burma say that he was a perfectly normal young policeman. Perfectly normal young policemen in those days in Burma had a pretty exciting time of it. Life, in comparison to most lives lived in this island and elsewhere, was never dull. All Burma, both in its natural beauty and luxuriance and in its delightful people, forbade that.

The next stage might have been dull, or sounded so. For one of the sounds which made up young George Orwell's days from now on was the clatter of his typewriter. Day after day, month after month, he sat making these sounds, often in an upper room of his sister's house near Leeds. For a writer learns by practising his craft, like any other artist. Writing and scrapping it, writing and scrapping it and emptying the wastepaper basket is the hard and necessary routine, the long road to the perfection of *Animal Farm*.

Very soon he had to earn his living. His leave pay could

be eked out for a year. This gave him a year's grace in which he could bang his typewriter and see if it produced enough for food and clothes and shelter. It failed him. It has never been easy for a beginner who insists on writing well to make enough money out of writing.

The books that he published tell us the little that we know of what happened in the years between his return and the publication of *The Road to Wigan Pier*. That was the first of his books to make some noise in the world and from then on plenty of people noticed him and have told us what he was doing. *Down and Out in Paris and London* tells us that he lived in Paris for some time, eventually in great poverty and hardship, at one time washing dishes in an hotel for a living, as some young writers today have been known to do in London under far easier conditions. Much of the Paris story is gay and amusing and is told with a lightness and charm that is not seen again in Orwell's writing until *Animal Farm*. It is only when the story returns us to London that the grit and grime, which Orwell loved so strangely, spreads over the scene.

For some reason that no one has been able to explain adequately, he wanted to be right down and out among the tramps. He said that he wanted to know how working people lived. It looks as if he never managed to live with working people but did manage the more easy jump right down among the classless outcasts whom anyone can join by just having the courage to do so. Tramps are not working people and in that way are more like the aristocracy, for they toil not, neither do they spin, and they do not worry about it. But unlike the aristocracy, tramps have no sense of social responsibility. They have no feelings about the herd, except a desire to avoid it. Orwell had an exaggerated sense of social responsibility and it must have been a relief to share for a while the outlook of people who had none.

But his serious intention was to find out how the other half of the nation lived, for he was living in the bad days of twenty or thirty years ago when class feeling was strong. He managed to meet a few of the working class as he tramped the roads of England from one Poor Law house to another. For he was walking in the bad days of slump and unemployment, the memory of which haunts older English workpeople still. Many a fine young man in those days, through no fault of his own, could not get work and could not support himself. Orwell tells us about some of them, individuals he happened to meet among the thousands of tramps constantly on the move in England then. That has all changed now. There are very few tramps and unemployment is apparently under control.

The years went by and Orwell went on trying to discover how working people lived. In ordinary times he might have been able to get a working class job. If he were serious in his desire to know what it felt like to be in a workshop or factory for eight hours or more a day, he might have been able to join a trade union and get a regular job. But in those days it would not have been fair and probably not easy to compete with a genuine worker. So George Orwell took casual jobs.

In his novel *A Clergyman's Daughter* he tells us about hop-picking, about being out of work and sleeping out in Trafalgar Square, and about teaching in one of those little private schools which have now been cleared away. In that twisted way he had, when he got a job in the teaching profession, he got a job in the shabby end of it, in a shaming little sector of it which has now disappeared. In his next novel, *Keep the Aspidistra Flying*, when he gets a job in a bookshop it is a poor sort of bookshop with a twopenny library of trash connected with it. In actual life this time, he had worked in a pleasant secondhand bookshop near Hampstead Heath. He had hired a room above the shop and when he could not pay the rent he worked in the shop. It was a strange life and he probably could not have lived it so or wanted to live it so in any but these sad and hectic decades between the wars.

It was now 1936 and he had published four books. Not a large output for almost ten years. None of them had been very successful and the author had only a small reputation. He had however acquired for himself quite a reputation in the description of dirt and squalor and when a publisher wanted a description of unemployment in the north it was entirely natural that he should commission George Orwell to write it. When *The Road to Wigan Pier* was published Orwell's name began to be heard of in the world.

In order to write the book he went north and lived there to see what was going on. The first part of the book describes what he saw. Once again he failed to live and work with working men. He lived in a cheap lodging which is described in nauseating detail and he went about finding dirt and decay both in men and the works of men. All this he described with relish but much the best two chapters of the book are about miners at work, hard at work, on the coal face.

The second part of the book is quite different. It is the story of his own life and beliefs up to that moment in time. He tells the story of his life up to 1937 as the background of his beliefs. He is the angriest of angry young men. It is his last outburst before he came to maturity. For before the book was published Orwell had gone to Spain as a journalist, to cover the Civil War. Spain is a fine country and the people of Spain have as much human dignity as any people. Europe has many fine peoples, the Spaniards among them, and no one will wish to trouble them now by discussing the troubles of twenty years ago.

What we must discuss is the effect Spain had on George Orwell. The impression the war made was immediate. He forgot his journalism and joined in the fighting. The impression was as immediate as that experienced by the Oxford philosopher, R. G. Collingwood, who found the revolution had all the sincerity of an innocent desire that everyone should live well. Collingwood writes about the Spanish Revolution at the end of his *Autobiography*, in a passage that is well worth study when considering the descriptions in *Animal Farm* of people being deceived about public events.

Orwell joined a pathetically comic militia called the P.O.U.M. which had very little in the way of uniforms, equipment, weapons or ammunition. What it lacked in these ways it made up for in courage and idealism. In the harsh rocky Spanish mountains Orwell lived and fought with

Spaniards, Frenchmen, Belgians, Italians and Germans. At last he was among working men. At last he belonged to a fraternity who were the salt of the earth.

He was badly wounded in the end and eventually brought back to Barcelona, that wonderful city which is the capital of the Catalonians. The Russian communists were at that moment taking charge, fighting it out with the Government troops who were fighting General Franco. Orwell and his friends were in great danger. His wife was there and he had to make plans for both of them to escape. Before he left, he heard that one of the leaders of his battalion, a Belgian engineer and professional soldier, was under arrest. He risked his own freedom and safety to visit his friend in gaol and do all he could for him before he and his wife finally escaped.

The book he wrote about it all, *Homage to Catalonia*, is one of his best. It is completely different in mood from the angry, bitter writing of *Wigan Pier*. He is still able to be angry and bitter, especially about the cynical Russian power politics in Spain. Chapter Eleven is about their propaganda methods in Spain and the reader will enjoy all the better Orwell's account of how the pigs used propaganda if he reads that chapter in *Homage to Catalonia*. He is hot with anger about the English politicians and newspapers who told the English people stories about the causes of the Spanish War and fighting which were very different from the truth. Chapter Five is all about that.

In the rest of the book we find a new mood in Orwell personally, a mood of certainty about the values of life, a mood of peace which comes from knowing what life is about and what is man's place in the scheme of things. Out of war, man's greatest folly, Orwell found understanding and peace. He found peace with himself, he knew now where he stood. His brilliant mind was now mature, and settled a question while others were still debating. But the world remained full of enemies for George Orwell. Evil and stupidity are always with us and, like a preacher in the religious ages of Europe, George Orwell spent his time in exposing evil and showing up stupidity.

At the end of *Homage to Catalonia*, he speaks of what strikes anyone returning to England from some hot and barren southern land: 'the railway cuttings smothered in wild flowers, the deep meadows where the great shining horses browse and meditate, the slow-moving streams bordered by willows, the green bosoms of the elms, the larkspur in the cottage gardens. . . .' That is prose of affection and once again Orwell sought what he loved in Hertfordshire. He and his wife ran a village shop so that they had a place in the community and they kept a vegetable garden and hens. One of his most charming essays is about buying fruit trees in Woolworth's and planting them and caring for them, so that some day someone would enjoy the fruit. This is the countryside, most probably, of *Animal Farm*.

He continued to seek the simple life. That is one of the most attractive things about him. He lived in what we call an acquisitive society, whether we call it capitalist or a welfare state. In an acquisitive society man lives by acquiring things for himself: selfish gain is the driving power to make men work. He stood outside of that, as a true preacher must. Poverty for him meant freedom. When he wanted to go and do something, he had nothing to leave, nothing to break away from. At this moment, also, he was a tired man, recovering from a serious wound and from all the nervous exhaustion of a campaign.

Very soon he was writing again and before the war came he published another novel, *Coming Up for Air*. Like H. G. Wells, Orwell liked to put more into a novel than a story about characters. He liked to write about the society in which his characters lived. So *Coming Up for Air* begins with a long description which is very critical of Building Societies. Their enormous power was fairly new then. Later on, the book is taken up with the threat of war, which Orwell wanted people to realize more clearly. The Building Society theme turns into a nightmare picture of a vast new housing estate. Orwell saw that it was one of the most revolutionary things in England that men could now change the face of their own countryside very rapidly with their powers of building. So in this novel he was looking forward not only to war but to the technical revolution which has changed English lives enormously since the war.

Very soon the war came. Orwell tried to join the army, but he was already suffering from tuberculosis and there was no chance of his being accepted for service. Greatly discouraged, he joined the Home Guard when it was formed and soon became a sergeant. He was tall and spare and looked well in his uniform, but his technical prowess with the homemade weapons of the Home Guard was not particularly remarkable. He joined the B.B.C. and worked in the Indian Section. He was much admired and loved by his Indian colleagues and he was the life and soul of the fine broadcasting that went out to India. When Singapore fell, he began a weekly talk to Malaya, giving the news to anyone who could listen.

In the last winter of the German war he wrote *Animal Farm*. He was relaxed and rested. The acute danger of defeat was over. The enemy was exhausting himself in Russia and was being defeated in Europe. Success could be foreseen. For three years Orwell had enjoyed for the first time regular and useful employment among people of his own class and kind. He had had a rest from writing. All these things combined to his producing a little masterpiece. This he did, but he had difficulty in getting it published. It was obviously a satire of totalitarian rule, and most obviously of the Russian kind of totalitarian rule under Stalin. Russia was an ally and everyone admired her gigantic struggle against the German war machine. One publisher after another rejected *Animal Farm*. At last, he got it accepted and it was published as 'a fairy story'. The most brilliant satire of modern times appeared in the charming and appropriate disguise of a story for little children. Very soon children of all ages were enjoying it in many languages all round the world.

It was written in good humour, the only one of Orwell's books to be written in that vein. The same good humour dominated the essays he wrote at this time. The nearest in spirit to *Animal Farm* are the little essays he wrote for *Tribune* while he was its literary editor. As soon as the German war was over he had left the B.B.C. and worked for *Tribune*. The little essays may be found at the end of *Shooting an Elephant* and they tell the reader a good deal about the author of *Animal Farm*. One probable reason for the special sweetness of these essays is that *Tribune* is rather a bitter paper and Orwell always found fun in being different.

These little essays, with the longer ones he wrote at the same time, stand with *Animal Farm* as his most interesting and mature work. *1984* is the work of a sick man, and the best things in that savage book are the two essays in it which were probably written at the same time as the group we have just been discussing. These are *The Theory and Practice of Oligarchical Collectivism*, and the appendix called *The Principles of Newspeak*, which for sheer brilliance surpasses any of Orwell's performances.

In *1984* Orwell's humour has evaporated. He is once again oppressed by the political evil in the world. He foresees a future of horror. It is different in one way from the horror which we really face as we approach the year 1984, for when he foresees endless conflict in mankind the weapons used are what are called 'conventional' weapons. There is no sudden universal explosion, for that would end his story of endless conflict before he began it. There is just endless fighting and endless shortages. The London of *1984* is often very like the London Orwell lived in during the last year of the war. The pains and torture are mostly mental and spiritual. Whoever wishes to study that kind of thing should supplement his reading of Orwell by reading Aldous Huxley's *Brave New World Revisited*.

Orwell was a dying man when he wrote *1984* and he was by now famous and a name. He escaped from the publicity of fame in typical fashion by going to live in a little island in the Hebrides. The climate was benign and the island was very beautiful and his last terrible book was completed. Rapidly, his health grew worse and he came back to England and lived in a sanatorium. Right up to the end he hoped to get better and he was planning to go and live in Switzerland when he died quite suddenly in January 1950.

It was a good life. He had made up his mind as a little boy that he wanted to be a writer and he expected his writings then to make £100,000. He became a writer and a famous one and his writings have affected English thought and speech more than anyone else's in his generation. Like so many writers, he was not content to be merely amusing. He wanted to make his readers think, he wanted to prick their consciences, he wanted to point out the way he thought they ought to go. He succeeded Bernard Shaw and H. G. Wells in his own generation. He wanted all human beings to be kind and sensible. He exhorted them in essays and stories, and in none of them does he do it more amusingly or to better advantage than in *Animal Farm*.

II. 'ANIMAL FARM'

We all know that a sheep is tame, a fox cunning, a rabbit timid and a dog faithful. It is their nature and when we read animal stories we expect the animals to behave according to their natures. It is enough if they do so. We are sufficiently amused.

Animal stories can be made in another way. The animals still behave according to their natures but they are also seen to behave just like human beings who happen to have the same natures as the animals. We say that a man is foxy, a boy a perfect rabbit and some wretched fellow an absolute pig. This kind of writing appears all over the world in every language and it has been common among English storytellers for hundreds of years. Chaucer's story of the cock and his hen, told by the Nun's priest nearly six hundred years ago, shows how amusingly it can be done. Chanticleer is frightened by a dream and tells his wife Pertelote. She upbraids him for his cowardice, and I quote the lines in the translation by Nevill Coghill:

All women long—and O that it might be!—

For husbands tough, dependable and free,
Secret, discreet, no niggard, not a fool
That boasts and then will find his courage cool
At every trifling thing. By God above,
How dare you say for shame, and to your love,
That anything at all was to be feared?

That is high comedy and the essence of it is that it is a hen talking to the cock.

Very often such stories are told with a didactic purpose. The fables of the poet Gay (first published in 1728) are a good example of telling an amusing story or recording an amusing conversation in order to point a moral, to instruct by pleasing. Beasts speak and act according to their natures and at the end a moral is drawn. For example, in one fable a shepherd's dog tried to reason with a wolf. Why should such a brave animal as a wolf attack sheep? Why not attack the bear and lion instead? Surely the wolf is a great soul and no coward? The wolf replies that nature designed wolves as beasts of prey and like every other creature, wolves must eat. If the dog is so excited about the wickedness of killing sheep, why does he not talk to his master, who is always killing sheep while, after all, a wolf only kills one now and then. And Fable XVII ends, as is customary, with the moral:

A wolf eats sheep but now and then,
Ten thousand are devoured by men.
An open foe may prove a curse,
But a pretended friend is worse.

Very neat, and it is safe to say that when the *Fables* of Gay are read nowadays it is because they are witty and neatly written.

Animal Farm has all the virtues and intentions of the animal story. It is a story about a society of birds and animals, each behaving according to its nature. It is amusing to see a cat so feline, a raven so ravenous and sheep so sheepish. On another plane, it is sympathetic to see that animals are so like humans: to see a willing carthorse behave so like any willing strong labourer, to see a young mare behave so like any conceited girl.

On a further plane, the emergence of the pigs as rulers of *Animal Farm* is the most damning indictment in an English story of the lust for power which overcomes men and is seen at its worst today in totalitarian societies. The animals in this story are all domestic animals who are disciplined as men are in civilized societies. They are therefore open to the same danger as men are in civilized societies. They are law-abiding and want peace and they get into the hands of harsh and ruthless rulers. These are the reasons why this simple story has raced round the world in so many languages. Truly civilized men hate brutality and ruthless force and if they can do nothing else about it they can relieve their feelings by enjoying a story which mocks it.

This mockery or satire is one ingredient of the story's success. It is the seasoning; but the main thing is the story itself. We all love a story that carries us away and this story carries us away so easily that we can read it right through without asking how it could possibly have happened. We recognize the setting. It is the Hertfordshire where Orwell lived and wrote and tended his garden and kept poultry. We recognize Farmer Jones and all the other country folk that came into the story. They are anything but typical because there isn't a nice man among them, and anyone who lives in Hertfordshire will find the country folk there as charming as country folk anywhere. The only way they run to type is that they are typical Orwell humans, cheap and nasty.

The natural setting is the south of England but it is not stressed at all and nothing is made of natural scenery in the story. It is all well in the background. Many of the facts of ordinary life are kept well in the background and even right out of the story. Why did Farmer Jones not send for the police? How did the animals pay the rates? Why did the county agricultural authorities not step in? In what language did the pigs do business? If the writer is skilful, we easily ignore these questions and they may not even occur to us at all. Orwell told his story with such relish and skill that, as the phrase goes, we willingly suspend disbelief.

If in this sense the story takes us right into the world of fantasy, in the satirical sense it is altogether too true. As a critical comment on human society and on the rulers of mankind, it is plain, stark, bleak truth. As a picture of the black arts of persuading people against their better judgement, of propaganda as we call it, it is a most useful and powerful warning. Keep the truth away from the people, this satire says, and tell your lies boldly and persistently and people can be made to believe anything. Orwell was obsessed with the dangers and potentialities of propaganda ever since he had seen it work in the Spanish war: 'I saw great battles reported where there had been no fighting, and complete silence where hundreds of men had been killed.' During the Second World War he was engaged in the B.B.C. in fighting propaganda and trying to get the truth across to India and the Far East. This strengthened his horror of public lying.

These strong feelings of his are expressed with great force and power in *Animal Farm*, but the book does not remain in our memories as an angry satire. It is a friendly story about animals and we may remember that one of Orwell's friends said it was not strange that this was the only really happy book Orwell wrote. When he wrote about people he was angry, scathing and ashamed. But he loved animals, and when he wrote about them his book is warm with friendly amusement. So in the end, the best way to read *Animal Farm* is not for the comments and the lessons but for the story and the characters. Like so many stories, this one consists mostly in different characters affecting one another. As so often happens, the worst come out on top. That is one way in which good characters become even better, by enduring the worst. Orwell enjoyed the company of good characters, and as much as anyone I ever met he got immense fun out of watching bad characters. It was only when he had his pen in his hand that most characters became bad and had a bad time of it. Let us look more closely at both kinds in *Animal Farm*.

The Characters: Animal

MAJOR: the old pig who provides the political philosophy on which *Animal Farm* is founded and the song which becomes their inspiration. Men, he tells the animals, are the only enemies. They steal all that the animals produce and make the animals work entirely for human profit. Get rid of men and earth will become a heaven for all animals. He offers the plausible idealist philosophy on which revolutions are based. If people are going to revolt, they must not see goodness or usefulness in the other side.

SNOWBALL: succeeds Major as the intelligent leader. He is dedicated to the revolution and to the betterment of animals. He is not only a good thinker, but a good general. He plans the battle and he fights bravely himself. He is defeated in the battle for leadership by Napoleon, who relies on cunning and brutality, and he is eventually chased into exile.

NAPOLEON: wholly committed to seizing and keeping power, and does so in the way of totalitarian leaders as we have seen them in Europe. He outwits Snowball because Snowball thinks of the good of their animal society and Napoleon thinks only of getting power. Napoleon plans far ahead and waits while the pups grow and are trained into the equivalent of storm-troopers or secret police. He keeps his power by propaganda, false information and opinions which are spread about for him by Squealer.

SQUEALER: 'a small fat pig' who 'was a brilliant talker' and 'could turn black into white'. He is the Public Relations Officer for Napoleon, his propaganda chief. It is Squealer's business to keep the animals in order by finding out what they are thinking and changing their thoughts when necessary. When they are puzzled by any order, Squealer explains it and persuades them to obey. When they become rebellious, Squealer frightens or cajoles them into obedience. He works all the time on the easiest of them, the sheep, so that there is always an obedient mass of opinion that can be relied on to shout for authority. He relies greatly, as all propagandists do, on the short memories of the creatures he is working on. The animals find it difficult to remember the details of the first fight, when Snowball led them; or what the Seven Commandments originally said. Squealer helped to rule the animals by using all the tricks that words and thought can be used for, and he is frightening and unpleasant unless we choose to regard him as very amusing.

BLUEBELL, JESSIE and PITCHER: are the three dogs whose purpose in the story is to produce the nine enormous dogs which are Napoleon's bodyguard.

BOXER: is the big, powerful farm horse who represents the simple, honest, strong and devoted worker. As the sheep represent the gullibility of the worker, Boxer represents the goodness of the common man. When Orwell said in *1984* that the hope of the world lay in 'the proles', he was thinking of people like Boxer, the salt of the earth. Boxer has few brains and he simplifies all problems into the need for working still harder for the cause he believes in. He is the worker of the world, on whom in the end all societies depend. When he is old, he is cast aside. He is sold as horseflesh instead of being given the pension the pigs promised all the animals. He had been heroic in battle and faithful to the cause all his days, and he gets the reward these virtues so often bring, not only in Orwell but in life itself.

CLOVER: the stout, motherly mare.

MURIEL: the white goat, who is hardly used in the story at all. Orwell may have meant to develop her place in the story, but it went otherwise. Her chief moment is in reading out the amended commandments to the others. She was no fool, and if Orwell had developed her, she would have been one of the two characters, the other being Benjamin, where Orwell departed from the traditional characters given to animals.

BENJAMIN: the donkey. Wise and silent. Cynical. More than any other animal he sees through the pigs and realizes the folly of trying to fight them. He is the intellectual character, who normally rejects fuss and demonstration, but sees what is going on more clearly than most people. He had Orwell's own ability to recognize political truth and its consequences far ahead of other people. Only once does he forsake cynical inaction and that is when his friend Boxer is betrayed and is being taken off to the slaughter-house instead of hospital. At once he rushes to save his friend, and inspires the animals to attempt a rescue. It fails, and Benjamin relapses into cynical observation. In Benjamin's character, as in Muriel's just noted, Orwell abandons the usual character given to animals. Benjamin is no donkey in the usual sense. It is in character for Orwell to contradict common error and in these two characters, as he draws them, the common idea of a goat or a donkey becomes quite wrong.

MOLLIE: 'the foolish, pretty white mare' who is quite incapable of serious thinking and whose whole idea of life is to be well fed and attractively adorned. She soon escapes from the rigours of *Animal Farm*, and she may be taken as a caricature of the soft bourgeois escapee from a revolution.

THE CAT: not even named, but a typical inhabitant of any farm. Is always there when there is food and then disappears for long intervals, especially when there is bustle or trouble. Lives an entirely private life and contributes nothing to the animal society, of whose efforts and intentions she seems to be entirely unaware.

MOSES: the tame raven, who represents the priesthood in a revolution. He also disappears in hard times and comes back when times are better and he can enjoy special privileges when food and drink are shared out.

The Characters: Human

MR. JONES: the owner of Animal Farm, which in his day was called Manor Farm. Mr. Jones had been a capable farmer but a lawsuit had depressed him and taken all his money. He lost interest in his farm, let his workers get slack and took to drink. This deterioration of the humans on the farm is necessary so that they could be chased away by the animals. The rebellion came at midsummer and only in October did Jones try to get his farm back. In the fight, he is frustrated by Snowball's tactics. Thereafter, his place in the story is as a bogeyman. If the animals thought of shirking work or rebelling against pig rule, it was enough for Squealer to say 'surely there is no one among you who wants to see Jones come back?' At the beginning of Chapter Ten we learn that Jones had died in an inebriates home in another part of the country. Like all the human beings in the story, Jones is shadowy and unpleasant.

MR. PILKINGTON: was one of the two neighbouring farmers. He was a gentleman farmer who neglected his work and spent most of his time hunting and fishing. When Napoleon asked Mr. Pilkington for help when Frederick attacked Animal Farm, he had already double-crossed Mr. Pilkington. So Mr. Pilkington did not attempt to help but sent a message: 'Serves you right.' In the last scene, however, it is Mr. Pilkington who proposes the toast to Animal Farm. The old conservative gentleman has come round at last to accepting the revolution, and his speech is a delicious caricature of political oratory.

MR. FREDERICK: owned the other neighbouring farm. He was very unlike Mr. Pilkington and that had to be so or the two farmers would soon have agreed to make an end to this animal experiment. Mr. Frederick was the tough, shrewd, hard-bargaining working farmer who is not unduly deterred by honesty. It was he who arranged to buy the timber from Napoleon and paid him in forged notes. It was he who attacked Animal Farm and blew up the windmill.

MR. WHYMPER: another unsavoury character. A solicitor who acts as go-between for the pigs in their business transactions with farmers and dealers. The man of law is rarely a favourite character in fiction. Somebody had to be the middleman between pigs and humans and Orwell makes him as unpleasant as his shadowy existence allows.

NOTES

*The notes in this edition are intended
to serve the needs of Overseas students
as well as those of English-born users.*

CHAPTER I

PAGE

1 *pop-holes:* small openings cut in the walls of the hen-houses, so that one bird at a time can get out or in.

Middle White boar: there is something about this breed that makes the boars look truculent and aggressive. Orwell was an acute observer and no doubt chose his breed carefully.

Willingdon Beauty: 'prize' animals (those carefully bred from selected high-grade parents) are each usually given a special name, just as racehorses are, to help make record keeping easy.

ensconced: comfortably settled; established.

had . . . grown rather stout: a polite English way of describing an animal (or a man or woman) who has become fat and bulky.

tushes: tusks.

2 *had never quite got her figure back:* an idiomatic phrase usually applied to a woman who has not recovered her slender youthful appearance after the birth of a child.

eighteen hands: a 'hand' as measurement of the height of a horse is four inches.

cynical remark: the kind of comment made by a speaker who has (or thinks he has) no illusions about life or human behaviour. From *Cynics*, a school of ancient Greek philosophers founded by Antisthenes in the 5th century B.C.

paddock: a small field where horses rest and feed.

filed: walked one behind the other.

2 *cheeping:* see note to page 8, below, on *lowed*, etc.

trap: a small and light two-wheeled open carriage; sometimes called a *dogcart.*

mincing daintily: walking in an artificial, affected, and conceited manner.

flirting her white mane: shaking or tossing it with a sudden movement to attract admiration.

the cat: the several references Orwell makes to the cat do not give it a very good character, but they seem to be made in playful, even affectionate, fun. See also above, page 104.

3 *the strange dream:* Major said he wanted to tell them his dream. Curiosity attracted them all to the meeting. Major gave them a political speech, promising to tell them about the dream later. Having held his audience in this way, at the end he said he could not describe the dream and prevented any objection by singing a song. Orwell enjoyed these ironic touches.

our lives are miserable: cf. the classical statement of this theme by Hobbes (1588-1679), the philosopher: 'the life of man, solitary, poor, nasty, brutish and short' (in *Leviathan,* 1651, chapter 13).

the order of nature: he shows, as all revolutionaries show, that everyone could be well off if only everything was shared. The first stage of a revolution is frequently a tremendous fight for an ideal.

4 *Man is the only real enemy:* the existing order is the enemy and the enemy must be represented as wholly bad. There is nothing in Major's speech about man feeding and tending the animals, building houses for them, putting down straw, looking after them when they are sick and so on. The enemy can have no virtues. Man is no more than the exploiter of all animals.

their natural span: the number of years they would probably live in the right natural conditions.

scream your lives out: all pigs by law must now be painlessly stunned by electricity before being slaughtered.

5 *You, Boxer:* in a satire of this kind, the memory must glance backwards and forwards to enjoy all the fun to the full. Major tells Boxer that Jones will sell him to the knacker. In fact, it is the pigs who do so, for the pigs behave like men, only they are more ruthless to their own kind.

knacker: a man who buys old horses and slaughters them to sell as food for other animals.

Only get rid of Man: the idea behind a revolution has to be simple. The people who preach the simple idea are those who betray it. The pigs became more ruthless rulers than men.

All animals are comrades: this sentence is the climax of a paragraph of huge mis-statements. The lie is given to this last and biggest lie when the dogs behave according to their nature and chase the rats.

6 *I have little more to say:* Major has a great deal more to say though in few words. This paragraph is the first enunciation of the laws of *Animal Farm*, culminating in the first statement of the famous phrase: All animals are equal.

to resemble him: when you read the last sentence of the story, your memory will return to this phrase. We can call these echoes satirical reverberations, and there are quite a few in this paragraph.

do not adopt his vices: this is a warning which all reformers and revolutionaries need to keep in mind.

Beasts of England: this is the anthem of the Revolution of Animal Farm. It is probable that old Major believed what his song says. It is certain that the pigs found it necessary to ban it once they had taken over power. Orwell was no poet, but this is a very good song of its type, plain and forceful in its beat and rhymes as well as in its sentiments.

7 *'Clementine'* . . . *'La Cucuracha':* the former is an old and popular students' song; the latter a modern dance-band tune in South-American rhythmic style.

8 *lowed . . . whined . . . bleated . . . whinnied . . . quacked:*
these (with *cheeping*, page 2, above) are a few of the
many English *onomatopoeic* words, i.e. those that imitate
sounds which cannot otherwise be described.

CHAPTER 2

9 *Major died peacefully:* as in life, the philosopher of revolution dies peacefully and others put his ideas into action.
Snowball and Napoleon: the contrasting types who lead
revolutions, the one intellectual and sincerely working for
the people, the other, who always wins, who is hungry
for personal power.
Berkshire boar: Orwell knew his pigs and Berkshires are
common in his part of Herttordshire. They are large,
nearly all black, and aristocrats of the pig world.
porkers: young pigs, up to 115 lbs. Larger, they become
'cutters' and then 'baconers'.
a complete system of thought: another stage in revolutionary activity. The words or writings of the teacher,
Major, are taken and shaped, or twisted, into a system of
thought which will lead to revolution. They are then
taught and spread about as much as possible. Fascism,
Nazism and Marxism all worked in this way and they all
had to fight good sense and apathy of the kind expressed
by the animals towards their teachers.

10 *the badge of slavery:* this is a familiar phrase in the vocabu
lary of revolutionaries when they wish to express contempt
for some social habit or custom of their opponents.
Moses, the tame raven: represents the priesthood, who want
the existing order to go on and resist change. Sugarcandy
Mountain is a neat touch of humour, inventing in a single
word a heaven for ravens.

10-11 *Boxer and Clover:* like most simple workpeople, are easily
persuaded to believe revolutionary teaching when it is put
to them as the realization of the highest ideals of man.

11 *Windsor chair:* a wooden armchair of a pattern once common in English farmhouses. Farmer Jones's arrangements are old-fashioned. He had carthorses instead of tractors, for instance, and later on, in Chapter 5, Orwell says that the farm was old-fashioned.

Midsummer's Eve: the 23rd June in England, on the night of which it was an old custom to take part in intoxicating rites and noisy revels.

rabbiting: shooting wild rabbits.

News of the World: the Sunday newspaper with one of the largest circulations in Britain.

12 *carpet bag:* made from carpet, a material no longer used for this purpose; such bags were formerly used for carrying luggage when travelling; in the United States, *carpet-baggers* became a contemptuous nickname for Southerners after the Civil War of 1861-65.

Jones was expelled: here the reader must willingly suspend disbelief. In reality, Jones could easily have come back and if he had not, the county agricultural authorities would have had to take over. The animals could not have looked after themselves. But it is necessary for the story to suppose that the animals were left alone and carried on alone. So we are hurried along with pictures of vigorous action and we do not stop to think. In this way, it really is a fairy story.

The harness-room at the end: cf. the storming of the Bastille in Paris in 1789 or the sacking of the palaces in St. Petersburg (renamed Leningrad) in 1917.

castrate: farm animals intended to be used only for meat are operated on to prevent their producing offspring.

13 *knoll:* a small hill or hump.

gambolled: played about in a lively manner, jumping and leaping.

spinney: a small wood or group of trees.

butted: pushed violently (*to butt*, in ordinary usage, means to attack by running against with lowered head).

14 *horsehair sofa:* a long seat covered with material woven from horsehair; such sofas were fashionable articles of furniture in the Victorian period.

lithograph: a picture first drawn on a flat block of polished stone and then treated with water and ink before prints are taken from it on paper or cloth.

hams . . . were taken out for burial: because the animals regarded them as remains of the dead bodies of their former comrades. A *ham*, in this sense, is the thigh of a pig, dried and smoked, ready for cooking.

stove in: a popular variant of *stave in* : smashed and broken open (of a cask, barrel, etc., made of *staves* = curved pieces of wood).

as a museum: humans have a strong sense of history, and some of these same palaces in Leningrad are preserved in this way.

15 *Snowball climbed:* note that it was Snowball who succeeded Major as intellectual leader and that his Seven Commandments really were based on Major's teaching. It was another hand, Napoleon's, that debased them.

Whatever goes upon two legs. this would ban birds, so the second commandment specifically says 'or has wings'.

No animal: the negative commandments are confined to those commandments in Major's teaching which Snowball and the other pigs believe they will never want to break. Part of the ironic amusement of the story is to see them all broken.

16 *mash:* corn, etc., soaked or crushed in hot water (or boiled) to serve as food for poultry and animals.

'Never mind the milk': from the first, Napoleon is full of self-interest, while Snowball thinks for the community.

CHAPTER 3

mowing and raking: cutting grass and gathering it into heaps before carting it away.

16 *bits:* rounded metal strips placed in a horse's mouth and attached to the reins with which the rider or driver guides and controls it.

17 *Gee up . . . Whoa back:* exclamations shouted to a horse, the former to start or hasten it, the latter to slow it or bring it to a standstill.

There was no wastage: the early, idealist days of revolution.

went like clockwork: a metaphor used to indicate anything that has proceeded smoothly and easily, and without interruption.

worthless parasitical human beings: the common language of revolutionaries. Masters are parasites, living on the people.

when they harvested: one of the few efforts in the story to explain logically how the animals got on without machinery.

cockerels: young male fowls.

18 *setback:* discouragement; a turn for the worse; interruption or reversal.

'Donkeys live a long time . . .': Old Benjamin means that they live long enough to see the consequences of rebellion and to expect little from it; and, consequently, that they are careful to keep out of trouble that might soon turn them into dead donkeys.

cryptic: puzzling.

19 *the Meeting:* a regular feature of the big collective farms in the early days of the Russian revolution. These committees did two things; they helped the people to learn to run their farms, and they helped people to find out where they were after the turmoil of revolution. Nothing in Pasternak's novel *Dr. Zhivago* is more moving than the picture of the middle classes after the Russian revolution slowly realizing there was no structure in society on which they could lean, no law to which they could appeal. These committees had virtue in them and when Napoleon seized power, he did away with them at once.

20 *faculty:* mental ability.

maxim: motto, slogan.

'Four legs good, two legs bad.': it is part of the irony that Snowball's statements are all contradicted under Napoleon's leadership later.

21 *propulsion . . . manipulation:* forward movement . . . movement or action performed with the hand.

whelped: whelp is an older word for *puppy* or new-born dog.

The mystery of where the milk went: in the course of a few pages Orwell carries on the revolution from the abundance stage to the shortages stage. At first, shortages occur in favourite foods like milk and apples, which the pigs greedily devour, and Squealer explains it quite simply: milk and apples 'contain substances absolutely necessary to the well-being of a pig'.

22 *this has been proved by Science:* Though science is, properly, concerned only with exact knowledge, opinions expressed by scientists are often quoted to support theories which politicians and others find convenient.

CHAPTER 4

23 *flights of pigeons:* propagandists for world revolution.

tap-room: that part of an inn or public-house where customers sit to drink beer and other beverages drawn through the taps; now more usually called *bar* or *saloon*.

its pastures worn out: through neglect, the ground had become incapable of producing good grass (pasture) for the animals.

These two disliked each other: A revolution succeeds to some extent because neighbouring countries fail to agree about putting it down. The statements which follow about the whole thing being over in a fortnight and about the terrible wickedness that flourished are echoes of world reaction to the Russian revolution. Orwell was a schoolboy when it happened and he was very interested in all he heard about it.

24 *cannibalism:* the eating of its own kind by any animal (or human being).

in common: belonging to the whole community, not to any individual.

tractable: easy to manage; docile.

refused their fences: a phrase used of racehorses and those used in fox-hunting which refuse to jump over hedges, gates, ditches, or any other obstacles they are expected to clear.

smithies: workshops where blacksmiths carried on their trade, making horse-shoes, farm implements, etc.

25 *an old book of Julius Caesar's campaigns:* probably a translation of Caesar's own famous *Commentaries,* which give an account of (mainly) his conquest of Gaul and Britain.

Snowball launched his first attack: Snowball fought and won the victory by his skilful conduct of the battle. Later on, we shall see how the pigs persuaded the animals that it was Napoleon who won the victory. In *Homage to Catalonia* Orwell says: 'I saw great battles reported where there had been no fighting, and complete silence where hundreds of men had been killed . . . it gives me the feeling that the very concept of objective truth is fading out of the world.'

muted: discharged their droppings.

skirmishing: brief fighting on a small scale.

26 *fifteen stone:* 1 stone = 14 lb.

stallion: a male horse kept mainly for breeding.

gored: pierced by an animal's horns.

ignominious: shameful, humiliating.

27 *The only good human being is a dead one:* In wartime the people of any one fighting nation are apt to hold an exactly similar opinion of their enemies.

impromptu: not previously planned; spontaneous.

27 *Animal Hero, First Class:* This is Orwell's satirical hit at titles and medals and especially at the Russian Soviet's giving high-sounding titles to citizens commended for political, military, artistic, or other services to the State.

horse-brasses: small ornamental plates, like medals, used to decorate harness. Genuine old ones are now collected as 'antiques'.

posthumously: after death.

CHAPTER 5

28 *pretext:* excuse; pretence.

paw the ground: scrape it with a hoof, foot, or paw.

word of honour: to 'give one's word of honour' is supposed to be a solemn guarantee that the truth has or will be spoken, or that some promised act will really be carried out.

29 *dogcart:* see note to page 2 above: *trap.*

forelock: hair hanging down the forehead.

manifestly: obviously; beyond question.

acreage: extent; an *acre*=4,840 square yards; 640 acres= 1 square mile.

successful with the sheep: i.e. organizing the masses on his side in the power struggle.

in and out of season: an idiomatic phrase applied to things done or said without reference to whether or not they are suitable or appropriate at that particular time.

30 Farmer and Stockbreeder: a weekly journal for farmers.

silage: grass or other greenstuff preserved in a pit or air-tight container (called a *silo*) until it is required as food for farm animals

basic slag. a waste product obtained during the making of steel; though it is useless there, it contains chemicals which are valuable to farmers and others when it is put into the ground as a fertiliser.

30 *windmill . . . dynamo . . . electrical power:* one of the first problems in backward communities is providing machinery for power to run other machines.

incubators: apparatus for hatching eggs and rearing chickens in a favourable and artificially maintained degree of warmth.

31 *closeted:* shut in for study or conference.

deeply divided: on the old problem of agriculture versus heavy industry.

slogans: brief easily-remembered phrases used by advertisers and propagandists. Though the word *slogan* is often regarded as modern slang, it is actually of ancient and respectable origin, signifying originally a Scottish war-cry.

33 *Snowball's eloquence had carried them away:* the quarrel between Snowball and Napoleon ranged over foreign policy (how to keep out the farmers), the economy of the farm and long-term planning (the windmill). Napoleon won because he had the sheep to bleat for him (like the disciplined cheers at Nazi rallies) and the dogs (or storm troopers).

34 *Afterwards Squealer was sent round:* Squealer at once becomes the propaganda chief. Napoleon, the leader, withdraws and becomes aloof, like Big Brother in *1984*. Squealer, like sophists through the centuries, is appointed to make the worse appear the better reason, and to explain away all violent changes of policy, as on building the windmill. He is Orwell's most effective picture of a propagandist.

35 *'Napoleon is always right':* one of the most pathetic aspects of human society is the blind following of unworthy leaders by humble folk.

The skull of old Major: cf. the exposure of the mummified body of Lenin in Moscow.

36 *manoeuvre:* (in the present sense) trick.

38 *governess-cart:* a light two-wheeled carriage with seats on both sides facing inwards. Used in the past by rich people for their children, who could be easily watched by the governess accompanying them.

39 *arable land:* that on which crops for human food are grown, as distinct from pasture-land where animals feed.

40 '*Is it written down anywhere?*': it was only in Major's speech. This reliance of propagandists on quickly fading human memory is touched on at length in *1984*. On the practical question here, trading contacts eventually have to be made after any revolution. Human communities have to live and let live.

41 *but never . . . with both:* foreign policy often consists in playing off one country against another.

42 '*in a bed with sheets*': all the commandments are eventually amended in this way. Orwell skilfully designed them so that they could be added to and the meaning changed.

44 *Snowball!:* the smear campaign against Snowball's memory is now intensified and is a very good picture of how a reputation can be destroyed and truth distorted.

CHAPTER 7

46 *infanticide:* murder of newly-born babies.

47 *clutches:* (in the present sense) collections of eggs for hatching.

   Black Minorca pullets: young fowls, black in colour, from a breed which originally came from the Spanish island after which they are named.

   coccidiosis: a common and frequently fatal poultry disease.

48 *in league with:* in alliance with; united with (usually for some unworthy purpose).

49 *blood-curdling:* (metaphor) terrifying.

50 *formulate:* give clear expression to; set down or state plainly.
51 *categorically:* in a manner that cannot be disputed.
   Napoleon stood sternly: now comes the blood purge, so unpleasantly familiar under totalitarian rule.
52 *Without any further prompting:* these confessions are another feature of totalitarian rule. By the simple use of drugs and persuasion, it appears that human beings may be conditioned to say anything required of them.
53 *lumbering:* clumsy.

CHAPTER 8

56 *lists of figures:* cf. *1984*, ch. 4, 'the Ministry of Plenty's forecast had estimated the output of boots for the quarter at 145 million pairs. The actual output was given as sixty-two million. . . . Very likely no boots had been produced at all.'
57 *a black cockerel:* a symbol of consequence that would have been fantastic under the old rule of Farmer Jones. Upstart rulers require pomp and ceremony.
58 *swill-bucket:* pail for pigs' food of mixed liquid and solids (usually discarded scraps and dregs of human food).
   skulking: hiding in a cowardly way; sneaking about.
59 *terrible stories were leaking out:* each side tells terrible stories about the other, so that the psychological Iron Curtain has, as it were, two iron sides to it. No one would want to escape to a much worse place, so every care is taken on both sides to show that conditions are intolerable.
   making cocks fight: In the past this was a popular 'sport': pointed or sharp-edged weapons were fixed to their feet, and two fowls so armed (and trained for the purpose) were set to attack each other in a small enclosure, called a *cockpit*, until one was killed. On account of its cruelty, cock-fighting was made illegal in England.
60 *gander:* male goose.
   privy to: secretly aware of.

118

60 *deadly nightshade:* a wild plant with berries containing
the poison called *belladonna*.

61 *struck dumb with surprise:* a good example of the totalitarian power to switch propaganda or policy completely
without any warning. The masses are conditioned to
accepting the wildest changes.

63 *to rally:* to encourage or order to fight again.

64 *detour:* a roundabout (indirect) way from one place to
another.

65 *'That is our victory':* a neat and satisfying comment on
war and victory celebrations. After all the blood and toil
and pain, it is a victory to have what you had before.

66 *a case of whisky:* this passage is high comedy, with no
background of political satire to take away from its
refreshing joy. Napoleon had a hangover.

67 *Straw was laid down:* This was a common practice in the
past when traffic noises outside a house would be disturbing to a person seriously ill within.

CHAPTER 9

69 *A too rigid equality:* not only in rations, for it seems
impossible for all men in a society to remain equal.
Ambition drives men to leadership and personal advantage, cf. *1984*, in which the three great super-states 'had
the conscious aim of perpetuating *un*freedom and
*in*equality' for 'human equality was no longer a thing to
be striven after, but a danger to be averted'.

readjustment of rations: Orwell wrote his best pamphleteer-
ing essay on this abuse of language in 'The Principles of
Newspeak', the appendix to *1984*.

life nowadays was harsh and bare: cf. *1984*, Part 1, Section
V, the opening.

72 *stratagem:* a carefully prepared trick or ruse.

Moses the raven suddenly reappeared: as the orthodox

priests returned to Russia when the rigours of the revolution were over.

73 *something had happened to Boxer:* the death of Boxer
makes a short story in itself, which moves rapidly as each
animal acts in character. The callous indifference of the
pigs except to see that their lies are believed is matched
by the courage of Benjamin and the other animals in
attempting to rescue him. Even the stupidity of the
slaughterer's own horses becomes part of this miniature of
the virtues and vices of any human society. It transcends
satire because every reader is concerned by the betrayal and
death of Boxer.

75 *a low-crowned bowler:* a kind of hard felt hat with a
curved top rising only three or four inches above the brim.

<h3 style="text-align:center">CHAPTER 10</h3>

78 *an inebriates' home:* an institution for persons suffering
from excessive drinking of alcohol (whisky, gin, etc.).

79 *rheumy eyes:* eyes (usually those of very old people) that
discharge a watery fluid.
morose and taciturn: gloomy and silent.
filial: the relationship of a child to its parents.

80 *frugally:* simply and economically.
so many pigs: in human society, so many bureaucrats. One
of the greatest economic difficulties of our time, for the
more bureaucrats there are, the less they get done.
racked: searched exhaustingly, cf. *1984*, chap. 8, where
Winston tries to make the old man rack his brains for
memories of the old days.

81 *the unalterable law of life:* this seems to have been Orwell's
final view. It does not seem to be universally true. In
Western societies the standard of living of ordinary people
has risen remarkably since *Animal Farm* was written. It
is certain that if Orwell had lived to see the material
progress of the past decade he would have modified his

views, for the progress has been extraordinary. On the other hand, in some Eastern countries things are worse than they were and they were bad enough before. Most experts would quarrel with the word 'unalterable', for they would argue that it only requires a change of human nature to make all well. Indeed some experts argue that human nature is the one thing in nature that can be evolved into something better.

81 *All animals were equal:* it is the old storytelling trick. The reader hears that all is well and everything is quiet just before another astonishing change.

83-4 John Bull, Tit-Bits, *and the* Daily Mirror: two weeklies and a daily intended for popular consumption.

84 *rat-catcher breeches:* a garment which from the knees downward is very tight-fitting and well protected; so named from the time when they were worn by professional rat-catchers. Now they are mostly worn by sportsmen and farmers.

watered silk: material woven in such a way that it reflects light to form a pattern resembling ripples on water.

85 *felt it incumbent upon him:* felt it to be a duty.

It was a source . . . : a splendid parody of official speeches on international occasions. This is what Orwell called *doubleplusgood duckspeak* in 'Newspeak'.

misgiving: distrust.

licence: lawlessness.

a discipline and an orderliness: thus a revolution to show that all animals are equal becomes a tyranny in which the common animals are enslaved as never before.

86 *witticism:* feeble joke.

his various chins turned purple: men who eat and drink too much tend to develop fleshy layers below the natural chin, and these become discoloured by any strain on the blood vessels.

our lower classes: Orwell was extremely sensitive to class warfare, as may be seen in *The Road to Wigan Pier,* Part 2. There was a good deal of class feeling in the thirties and forties in England, much of it encouraged for political purposes. In the fifties, fortunately, it died down.

86 *bon mot:* smart remark; 'wisecrack'.

pampering: over-indulgent (or too soft) treatment.

clink his mug: the clinking (touching together) of drinking-vessels is a sign of comradeship and goodwill at social gatherings.

Nothing could be further from the truth!: if you want to tell a lie, tell a big one, as Hitler said. Describing Animal Farm as a *co-operative enterprise* was a truly Napoleonic lie.

title-deeds: legal documents necessary to prove a person's ownership of a particular piece of land (or a house, etc.).